UNCLE JOE'S SENPAI
ジョーおじさんの先輩

Micah Thorp

Touring rock bands
A father searching for his daughter
And a haiku master

For Sebastian, Alexander, and Morgan

Senpai 先輩 : Senior student, an upperclassman
who mentors an underclassman.

Ojisan おじさん : Uncle

CHAPTER 1

Uncle Joe's Band

We're Uncle Joe's Band screamin' out loud
We've got a rockin' metal sound
And a big rowdy crowd

—Uncle Joe's Band, *The Black Album*

Uncle Joe's Band was modestly successful. Able to play in modestly large venues, modestly filled with modestly interested patrons, they counted themselves successful, modestly. Three years after their breakout album had sold enough copies to garner some intermittent radio play, they achieved enough notoriety to open for more famous rock bands, attend various music award shows, and endorse an occasional household cleaning product.

The band's sound was both deafening and lyrical. A combination of explosive guitar riffs, driving bass, and combustible percussion, combined with strangely insightful, if not poetic lyrics, made even the most uninterested listener raise an eyebrow and wonder who had decided *that* band's music should be on the play list.

Once headquartered in a squalid house in Vallejo, California, their modest success had allowed the band to find more opulent quarters inside a renovated San Francisco loft complete with a small sound studio, bedrooms, an unused kitchen, and a large gathering space. Adorned with a combination of replica fine art and framed concert posters, the living space was comfortable. A silver refrigerator was kept well stocked with locally sourced organic meals, a variety of healthy vegetable drinks, and the occasional bottle of kombucha.

The band members could best be described as the human equivalents of refurbished mid-century furniture, once decrepit in the way things that have been overused are quickly worn out, now rebuilt to highlight the scars of their earlier years. Decades of excesses, late nights, drinks on the house, inebriated fans, and a virtual pharmacy of readily available illicit substances left the quartet with cirrhotic livers, emphysematous lungs, and sclerotic vasculatures. But despite their accumulated infirmities, the group maintained a creative spark, one that seemed to grow with time, such that when they recorded an album or took the stage for a show their collective presence allowed for the creation of something that seemed far in excess of their physical capabilities. Worn though they were, stirring the spirit and imagination of listeners occurred on more occasions than not. They had matured, both as people and as a musical ensemble.

Yet even in their greatest moments of creative triumph, the band, both individually and collectively, sought something else, something both ephemeral and permanent. Something that might sustain them when their own artistic passions had begun to fade. Something that might engender a sense of completeness, of whole, beyond what they could find in the invention of music.

And so, Uncle Joe's Band played on, night after night, in venues large and small, ever in search of a thing they could never quite articulate, ever seeking but never quite fulfilled.

––––––––––––

The doorbell buzzed several times before Steve managed to push the intercom and peered through the camera into the loft's entry. The doorbell had been fashioned to emanate the sound of an electric guitar riff, which seemed clever when the idea was conceived. In practice the sound of the doorbell proved grating, like the sound of a car engine that won't start. Thankfully the band members had become inured due to years of repeatedly hearing the same sound.

Steve squinted as he stared at the screen next to the intercom, filled with the face of a fifteen-year-old girl. Her brown hair was tied in a ponytail, and her black leather jacket and Doc Martens offset an otherwise soft appearance.

"Hey, Allison. Come on up. I'll see if your dad's awake." He pushed the open button next to the intercom and turned to yell toward the loft's bedrooms. "Hey, everyone! Allison's here!"

As if on cue, three of the bedroom doors opened and the remaining band members spilled out into the living area, disheveled and still somewhat somnolent, despite the late hour of the day.

Ian, the least sleep deprived of the group, was already dressed, a long-sleeved black tee and black jeans covering his long, thin frame. Wearing round Lennonesque sunglasses he appeared as though he might have just returned from clubbing or an evening ride on his Indian motorcycle. Yet in contrast to his eyewear, he held a porcelain cup in his left hand as though he were interrupted during his midday tea. "Bloody marvelous," he cooed with his usual wisp of Cardiff and Cockney. As the band's lead singer, he was the very embodiment both in the voice and manner of an English rock star, despite his upbringing in rural Western Michigan.

As Ian sat on the couch, Rick and Rod stumbled into the living space, each disheveled in their own unique way.

"Where is she?" Rick mumbled, his straw-colored hair falling over the black concert T-shirt he'd clearly been wearing for more than a day. As the Uncle Joe's Band's bassist, he exuded an odd confidence, despite his deep-set eyes and milky white skin, which under the best of circumstances gave him the appearance of a concert T-shirt clad vampire just arisen from his coffin for the evening.

In contrast to Rick, Rod's brown hair and round face was both uninteresting and average, the visage of someone who while unkempt, his appearance differed little from when he was well coiffed. Despite his bland appearance the group's lead (and only) guitarist was clearly excited. As he stepped near the couch where Ian had taken roost, his leg became caught on the coffee table and he fell headfirst into the floor. As if on cue, the door opened and Allison stepped into the room.

"There she is!" Steve shouted, throwing his tattooed, muscular arms around her, giving her a big bear hug. Allison hugged back.

Rick and Ian hugged her next, Ian carefully doing so while retaining hold of his cup of tea.

Rod pulled himself to his feet and practically bounced up to Allison as though he hadn't tripped and fallen on his left knee, now throbbing. "You look great! Any problems on the BART? How's school going? Are your grades good?" He paused to take a breath.

"Thanks, no, good, and yes." Allison kissed Rod on the cheek. "And it's good to see you too, Dad."

Uncle Joe's Band was configured in the manner of other classic rock and roll quartets. The band members included a drummer, Steve Sanchez; a lead (and only) singer, Ian Schwartz; a guitarist, Rod Nelson; and a bassist, Rick McMahon. The group spent years living in a squalid house in Vallejo, California, before realizing a contract with a record label. Shortly thereafter the band went on tour, released an album to a national audience, went on tour, took part in a music festival, went on tour again, cut a second album, and then went on yet another tour. Three years on, the group bore evidence of artistic exhaustion, capable of only modest creative production. Yet as much as they struggled, the desire to return to the road was ever-present. The roar of the crowd, the bright lights, the encores, seeing their faces on billboards and posters, the catered meals, and constant adulation left them all feeling more alive than any of them could remember.

The source of the band's inspiration, their creative spring, their muse, was Rod's daughter Allison. Following a period of confusion determining exactly which band member was Allison's father, a combination of ancestral detective work and awkward questioning finally led to the conclusion that Rod Nelson was Allison's father.

Allison dropped her backpack on the couch, skipped to the refrigerator, and opened the door. As she did the men watched and collectively held their breath. Inside were neatly stacked cardboard containers, each labeled with a carefully handwritten tag, organized based on their contents.

Allison touched a few of the boxes and turned back toward the band. "Looks like someone just stocked up on the quinoa salad." She smiled.

As if on cue the men exhaled. Rod pointed to a pile of cartons. "And we've been supplementing with the kale crunch bars."

Rick picked up Allison's backpack. "I thought we weren't buying leather."

Allison tilted her head. "It's fake leather. Can't tell, can you?"

Rick stroked the sides of the backpack and nodded. "It feels so real."

Ian flopped down on the couch. "What say we go for a quick spin on the bike?"

Allison flopped down next to him. "Do you still have my helmet?"

"Of course. The one with the shooting stars, if I'm not mistaken. Got it on a shelf in the garage."

Allison nodded.

"Well then, we'll run it out after lunch."

Steve scratched the top of his head. Over the preceding three years his male pattern baldness had worsened such that he had taken to wearing stocking caps on the top of his head. At times they itched. "How long do we have you for?"

"Two months."

The room grew quiet. Then a collective cheer rose from the four men.

———————

The name Uncle Joe's Band was an homage to Rod Nelson's Uncle Joe and the Grateful Dead's famed song "Uncle John's Band." Uncle Joe was a longstanding Deadhead who had chosen a life as a nomad, traveling from concert to concert in his beat-up Volkswagen bus. Never one to miss the opportunity to attend a concert, try a new mind-altering substance, or express his insights into nature, work, or the meaning of life, he wove his way through a cacophony of different places and events.

In the course of Joe's many travels he interacted with dozens, perhaps hundreds of similarly minded free-wheeling Grateful Dead fans. At concerts Uncle Joe was frequently met with waves, handshakes, "hey, Joe," "how's it goin', Joe," and "it's Joe, better hide your stash."

Near the end of his life, Uncle Joe had convinced his nephew Rod to start a band. The moment of conception occurred during a chance encounter between a young Rod and well-worn Uncle Joe at a Dead concert. Joe, at that point an acquaintance of Jerry Garcia, introduced Rod to the guitar master, who suggested that starting a band might be a meaningful life choice, should the opportunity arise. So, when Rod found he'd followed his uncle's advice and taken the initiative to start a band, he convinced his band-mates to name it after Joe.

Aside from the band, there is little of Uncle Joe's life that can be found in the annals of recorded history. The minor roles he played in numerous events throughout the 60s, 70s, and 80s were never announced, recorded, or for that matter, appreciated. Which is probably the way Joe would have wanted it. An ethereal being, his presence might be ascribed to an existence on a transcendental plane, one where lives are felt, rather than ascribed. Like a pebble dropped in a pond, whose ripples emanate even after the pebble disappears beneath the water's surface, Joe's life affected many, often in ways they could not see or even understand.

———————

Rod and Allison had gone out to get vegan pizza, Steve was visiting some friends in Vallejo, Rick was asleep in his room, and Ian was sitting at the kitchen table when Sy walked into the loft.

Ian looked up from his cardboard carton of veggie hash. "How did you get in? Did Steve give you a key?"

Sy set her motorcycle helmet on the table, her short black hair barely moving as she shook her head. "Who do you think it was that found this place for you guys?"

"So, you *do* have a key?"

"My name is on the lease. Yes. I have a key." She sat down matter-of-factly.

As the Uncle Joe's Band's agent and general caretaker, Sy was viewed with great reverence and suspicion. Younger than most of the band-mates, she was invariably unemotional and always direct. The band had learned that whenever she told the band they would or should do something, pushing back simply increased the likelihood they were going to do it.

Sy pulled out a chair and sat across from Ian. "I have some news for you. Are you the only one here?"

Ian looked around the room. "Bloody right."

"Well then, that's good, because I have something for you too." Sy pushed a white envelope across the table.

Ian opened the envelope and pulled out a typewritten note. He read it slowly, looked up at Sy, and then read it again. "Who sent this?"

"We don't know. As you can see it wasn't signed."

"How do we know if it's true?"

Sy drummed her fingers on the table. "We don't. It may simply be a piece of crazy fan mail."

Ian took off his sunglasses and read the letter a third time. He stood and set the letter on the table. "Bloody crazy. I don't know what to do with this."

Sy nodded. As she did Rod and Allison burst through the door.

"We have shirts," Allison said as she set a pile of folded multicolored T-shirts on the table. "They were selling them at the farmer's market to raise money to help relocate homeless cats."

"Houseless," Rod interjected.

"Right, I meant houseless. The farmers at the market take the cats back to their farms where the cats can live in barns and catch mice and have nice happy lives."

Sy's right eyebrow rose. "Isn't a cat living in a barn still without a house?"

Allison frowned, considering the semantics of whether a cat living in a barn was still houseless, even though it potentially had a home. After all, was the cat not homeless anymore even though it was still houseless?

Rod pointed to the letter on the table. "Fan mail?"

Ian shook his head. "No. And yes."

Before anyone could say anything else, Allison grabbed the letter. She stared at it for several seconds. "Oh my *God!*" She looked at Ian. "You've got a *daughter!*"

"Too." Sy interjected. "Too. As in also." She pointed at Allison. "Too."

Rod snatched the letter from Allison. "Does he? I mean this isn't even signed." He looked at Ian. "Do you know who sent this? Or why?"

Ian sighed. "No idea."

Sy stood up and took the letter from Rod. "Normally we'd ignore this sort of thing. But there was enough specific information about Ian we had to show it to him and ask."

As Sy set the letter on the table, a disheveled Rick entered the room wearing pajama bottoms and a Metallica T-shirt. His straw-colored hair was pulled up in a bun with several random strands falling off in various directions. He nodded at Sy and made his way to the coffee-maker. After shoving a cup under the dispenser and dropping a cartridge into the machine, he pushed a button and turned around.

"Ian has a daughter," Allison said, matter-of-factly.

Rick didn't respond; just stared straight ahead for several seconds as the coffee maker spurted dark roast into his cup. As the machine stopped, he turned, pulled out his cup, and began to drink. After he'd consumed half the cup, he looked up. "What's Ian's daughter's name?"

"We don't know," Sy replied.

"Then how do you know he has a daughter?"

"He got a letter. It's from someone who says she had spent several nights with Ian nineteen years ago. She says his daughter's in a band but doesn't mention her name."

"And it isn't signed," Rod added, handing Rick the letter.

Rick swallowed the rest of his coffee and read the letter. "Well, it has the name of the band."

Ian leaned back in his chair. "Isn't there some way we can do a DNA test or something? I mean if I have a daughter, it would be good to be certain."

Rod nodded. "Yes. It would definitely be good to be certain."

Rick put his cup back under the coffee-maker spout. "Why don't you look up the band and see if there's a nineteen-year-old girl who looks like you?"

Sy pulled a laptop out of her riding bag. She looked at Rick. "Good idea."

Rod, Allison, Ian, and Rick stood behind Sy as she sat at the table and began to tap keys on the laptop. After a moment she leaned back. "There it is. Stygian Teal."

Sy clicked through more search engine results. "They're local. It looks like they're playing at the Magenta Raven tonight. There isn't much more information about them. I can ask around and see what I can find out."

"Or we could just go see them," Rod replied.

Rick nodded. "Yeah, just go watch and see if the girl in the band looks like Ian."

Ian sighed. "This is a bloody lot. I don't know if I'm ready for this."

Allison patted him on the back. "You don't have to do the whole 'hey there, I'm your dad' thing. You can just watch and think about what to do next."

"Yeah, just go and do some fact-finding." Rick began to slurp more coffee.

Sy rolled her eyes. "Let's just take a brief pause before we go looking for Ian's potential daughter." She took a deep breath before continuing. "First, note the use of the word *potential*. We don't know what we don't know and right now that's a lot. So, let's not assume we are going on a search for a young woman who was unfortunate enough to have a philandering singer as her father. Secondly, as your business manager, agent, and general caretaker I can say this is a distraction and we have a tour that is *just about to start*. Finally, as an overtly decent human being I just have to say: Oh my God! Did your parents not teach you about safe sex? Are you not just a little concerned that you have children running around who you've fathered but never *actually* met?"

The room was silent for a moment when the loft door buzzed and Steve walked in the room. He looked at everyone. "What happened?"

Ian replied, "We're going to see a show tonight."

CHAPTER 2

The Color of the River Styx

Where the river runs red
Where the sky is gray, there is a place in the dark
Where the dead go to play

—Stygian Teal, "Swimming the Styx"

The Magenta Raven was a warehouse near the waterfront in San Francisco that had been converted into a black-lighted, audio-enhanced, disco ball, and chrome-encrusted dance bar. As the members of Uncle Joe's Band, Sy, and Allison approached the entrance to the bar, they made their way past a line of decidedly younger, better-dressed patrons. At the front of the line, they encountered a large bouncer.

Ian stepped forward. "Hi. We're Uncle Joe's Band, here for the evening." The bouncer looked at Ian and the rest of the band. "No." He turned back toward the next person in line.

Sy stepped forward. "Hey, excuse me." The bouncer ignored her. Sy pulled a card out of her jacket and pushed it into his chest. The bouncer grimaced and looked at the card. As he did his face changed. He looked at Sy for a moment and then stepped aside and motioned for the band to enter.

As they moved through the doorway Rick leaned toward Sy, "What did that card say?"

"Was a card from the company he works for. I have cards for all the security companies. Gets me into any venue anytime." Sy shot Rick a sly smile.

The interior of the Magenta Raven was a throbbing morass of bodies surrounding a stage. The stage was empty, but off to one side a DJ sat behind a table waving his arms. The room was lit with the glow of purple-black lighting and the occasional strobe light. Ian, Rick, and Sy made their way to a table.

"Where are they?" Ian asked and pointed at the stage.

As if on cue, the room went dark. The crowd grew quiet. Suddenly a light shone from the back of the stage. As it did the quiet groan of an electric guitar rang out. As the guitar riff gradually grew in volume a spotlight lit up the guitarist. She was thin and muscular with short dark hair and a black leather jacket. Her magenta-tinged guitar matched her mini-skirt and stockings, which were pulled over her high-top Doc Martens.

Ian looked at Rick. Over the noise of the crowd, he exclaimed, "She's a guitarist!"

As the guitar solo grew in volume the pulsating thump of a bass guitar began to rattle glasses on tables throughout the club. A second spotlight revealed the bassist. Like the guitarist, she had short dark hair and a black leather jacket.

Rick looked at Ian. "Or maybe a bassist."

A moment later the sharp rasp of drumming began. Ian took off his sunglasses and his eyes grew wide as a spotlight revealed the drummer, a young woman with dark hair partially dyed green, wearing a black tank top.

Ian held his breath such that the veins in his neck began to bulge. After a moment he let out his breath. As he did, a loud voice rang out. Stage lights illuminated the band, including a lead singer. She was a bit taller than the others and her hair was longer, pulled back in a ponytail, but like the others her hair was dark. She wore a black tee and black jeans. She began to sing with a low voice that rose to a near scream.

Sy tapped Ian's shoulder. "There are four of them. Four. Any idea which might be yours?"

Ian shook his head. "No idea, mate. No idea."

The opening song ended and the singer stepped forward. "I'm Jane. That's Sara on the drums, Indira on the bass, and Kara on the guitar. Together we are Stygian Teal." Jane raised a fist and the band started to play another song.

Rick and Steve nodded as Stygian Teal played the next few songs. Ian sat speechless, glasses off, eyes wide open. Sy and Rod slowly made their way through the crowd to get a closer look.

After several songs, Stygian Teal took a break and wandered toward the back of the stage. Sy and Rod made their way back to the table with Ian, Steve, and Rick.

Rod patted Ian on the shoulder. "Any idea which one is yours?"

Ian continued to stare straight ahead, eyes wide open, mouth agape.

Rod looked at Sy. "I think that's a 'no.'"

Stygian Teal finished their second set, took a bow, and huddled at the back of the stage. Throughout the dozen or so songs they played, Ian didn't move, staring, transfixed. The rest of the band and Sy watched the show with interest, every so often glancing at Ian, trying to ascertain whether he could tell which member of Stygian Teal was his progeny.

Rod and Rick quietly debated whether the drummer's nose was similar enough to Ian's to represent some sort of heritable trait, and whether any of Stygian Teal's band members reflected Ian's musical talent.

Sy remarked more than once that they were markedly better than she had expected and wondered aloud if they had representation.

At the end of the set Sy stood up and put her hand on Ian's shoulder. "Do you want to meet them?"

Ian's trance broke for a moment. "I'm not sure. Should I?"

Sy shook her head. "No. Don't think you're ready for that. I'll go chat with them, see what I can find out."

Rod raised his hand. "Can I come?"

Rick chimed in. "Me too?"

Sy rolled her eyes. "Fine. Let's go talk to them."

Stygian Teal were breaking down their. equipment when Sy, Rick, and Rod approached. Sy cleared her throat and the four young women stopped and turned toward her.

"Hi. I just wanted to tell you how impressed we were with your show."

The members of Stygian Teal nodded and turned back to their amplifiers, instruments, and mikes.

"Yeah, you guys were great." Rick tried to avoid appearing creepy as he smiled.

The Stygian Teal bassist mumbled, "Thanks".

Rod cleared his throat. "We're in a band too. Uncle Joe's Band. You might have heard of us."

The Stygian Teal band members didn't respond.

Sy shot a look at Rod. "Yes. They're in a band that has a contract with a recording label and I'm their *agent*."

In unison, Stygian Teal stopped and looked at Rick, Rod, and Sy.

The lead singer appeared to smile. "Oh, hi. I'm Jane. Nice to meet you." Jane stuck out her hand. "What groups do you represent?"

Sy responded with no hint of irony or emotion. "Gravestone, Mary's Pichard, Icing and Uncle Joe's Band, to name a few."

Jane nodded. "We've heard of Gravestone, Mary's Pichard and Icing."

Sy frowned for a moment before continuing. "What sort of sound are you going for? You seem very Sleater-Kinney."

"Thank you. We do mostly punk."

"Do you have representation?"

Jane looked at the bassist, Indira. "Not really. No."

Sy nodded and looked at Rod. "I'd like to hear more. How much original material do you have?"

The Stygian Teal guitarist cleared her throat. "We have several songs."

Sy didn't flinch at the response. "Well, I'd like to hear some of them."

Rod pointed at one of the amplifiers. "They could use our studio."

Jane looked at Rod. "Who are you guys?"

"Uncle Joe's Band."

Jane looked at the drummer and bassist who both shrugged. The guitarist looked at Rod. "'Broken Slipper?' I think you guys did that."

Rod smiled. "That was our breakout."

"And now we have a studio," Rick added.

Jane smiled for the first time. "Tell us when and where. We'll be there."

———————

Stygian Teal had to ring the loft doorbell several times before anyone answered. When the door finally opened, they were surprised by both the size of the loft and that all four of Uncle Joe's Band's members were there to greet them.

After brief, awkward introductions the bands retreated to the studio, a space nearly as large as the rest of the loft, meticulously designed and constructed, conveniently located behind the living space.

Throughout their tenure as musicians Uncle Joe's Band had performed in, lived in, traveled in, and slept in nearly every run-down, noxious roadhouse, hovel, motel, and shanty along the I-5 corridor. Despite these surroundings they had always managed to practice and record music in the most immaculate recording studios. Ever careful to ensure the proper acoustics and mixing equipment were used as they created and developed new songs, the band poured whatever meager resources they had into their recording spaces. The studio in the loft was no different. A large wood-paneled room covered with audio-absorbing panels, microphones, and various instruments was immediately adjacent to a small mixing room with a large soundboard. Behind the mixing room, a small office.

As they made their way into the studio, Stygian Teal was visibly impressed, despite their efforts to appear nonchalant. Steve, having missed the band's performance at the Magenta Raven, was particularly interested in meeting the female quartet. His eyes grew as he stared at four dark haired, not-identical-but-close-enough-that-anyone-one-of-them-could-be-Ian's-daughter young women. Allison was introduced as Rod's daughter. She sat and stared with a morbidly curious smirk on her face as the two bands met.

After the niceties concluded, Sy addressed the two groups. She pointed to the instruments in the room. "Okay, why don't you ladies show me what you can do?"

"Who's the drummer?" Steve asked as the Stygian Teal band mates looked at the instruments.

"Me. I'm Sara."

Steve cleared his throat. "Great. Well, just to warn you, the high Tom has a little extra vibrato. There are a couple extra sets of sticks behind the seat."

Sara sat on the stool behind the kit. "Is it okay if I raise the height of the stool?"

Steve stepped behind the kit and pushed a button. A motor hummed and the stool seat began to lower. Sara gasped in amazement.

Indira pulled Rick's bass from a stand and slung the strap over her shoulder. As she turned around Rick handed her the cord to the amplifier, which she plugged into the guitar. Rick tapped the neck. "This is Drago. And I'm Rick."

Indira smiled. "I'm Indira."

"Let's hear a few bars."

Indira started a slow A-G-D riff.

Rick reached for one of the keys on top of the guitar neck and turned the tuner ever so slightly. "The G is always off a bit."

As Indira played on the bass, Rod helped Kara, the Stygian Teal guitarist, hook her electric guitar to the studio's amplifier. When he tried to plug the cord into the guitar the end of the plug was too large.

Rod held up the plug. "Something's wrong. We may need a different cord."

Kara grimaced. "Oh, I forgot. My guitar has an updated plug. It works with Bluetooth."

Rod stepped back. "Bluetooth? You mean you don't need a cord to attach to the amplifier?"

Kara nodded. "That's right. But it only works with the right kind of amp. I didn't bring a regular cord with me."

Rod looked around. "Well, we can probably find you something to play with around here. We've got a couple extra guitars." As he turned to check a supply room in the back of the studio, Allison appeared holding a corral green Stratocaster.

"How about this one?"

Kara took the guitar from Allison. "This is really nice." She put the strap over her shoulders and caressed the neck. "Where did you get this?"

Allison smiled. "From my dad. Or dads."

Kara strummed the guitar's bronze-colored strings, and then pulled the body up to examine it. "What's this?" She pointed to the letters "JG" written below the pick-guard. Rod touched the lettering. "We don't know. I found it in my Uncle Joe's van after he passed away. We think it might be someone who owned it before my uncle, but no one's sure."

Allison rolled her eyes. "It's Jerry Garcia, duh."

Kara's eyes grew. "What? I'm holding Jerry Garcia's guitar. Whoa..."

Rod put his hands up. "Not necessarily. We really don't know where my uncle got this guitar, or why Jerry Garcia would sign it."

Allison shook her head. "It's obvious. Uncle Joe was a big-time Deadhead who never even played. Why else would he have a guitar with a 'JG' on it?"

"It makes a nice story, but we have no proof that it was the case. For all we know it might be John George, or Jimmy Green, or Josh Gerhard."

Allison looked at Kara. "It's Jerry Garcia. He'd want you to play his guitar. And please don't wipe off his initials." She turned and marched back to the sound room.

As Sara, Kara and Indira were getting set up and acquainted with their instruments assisted by Rod, Rick, and Steve, Stygian Teal's lead singer Jane sat in the sound room with Ian trying to appear unimpressed. She pointed to a framed concert poster on the wall. "Is that you guys?"

Ian peered at the poster as though he'd never seen it before. "Why yes, that's us. Was a show in Sacramento we did with the Basenjis. Was in an outdoor arena, very hot."

Jane nodded as though she too had similarly performed in outdoor arenas with other bands.

Ian sat in one of the control room chairs, trying not to appear inquisitive. "How did you come to be a musician?"

"My mother liked to sing in church. I wasn't a big fan of church but I liked to sing."

Ian nodded. "Quite bloody appropriate. Your father must have loved to hear you sing." He paused, hoping for an insightful answer.

Jane pointed to the mixing board. "How did you learn to use that?"

"Oh, it's all very complicated." Ian pulled his glasses down his nose. "Not really."

Jane smiled for the first time. "How do you guys come up with new music? I heard one of your albums on the way over here. It was pretty good." She paused. "You know, if you like metal."

Ian leaned back and crossed his arms. "It's all about the process, you know. All about how one goes into a mental state where they can see the song as the song wants to be. Where it lives and breathes. And then one must coerce it out. Out in the open where everyone can see and hear it." His eyebrows rose. "It's all a bit like giving birth, I suppose. Not that I have any *direct* experience with that, but if I had a child, let's say a daughter, it would be a bit like seeing her for the first time. Right there in front of you and you're so amazed at her you're not even quite certain what to say."

Jane took a deep breath and let it out. "Well, okay. I'm not sure I follow, but it sounds like a neat way to write music."

"And what sort of music do you write?"

"We've done a lot of different stuff, but we do our best when it's girl band punk. I write a bit of rock and hip hop, but mostly punk."

"What do your parents think of it?"

Jane laughed. "My mom thinks I'm possessed by the devil. But despite that she really likes it."

"And your dad?"

"Oh, I don't really know my dad," Jane quietly replied.

Ian took a deep breath. "Well, I'm sure he would like it very much. I have no doubt your music is bloody beautiful."

———————

When Stygian Teal was done setting up in the studio and tuning their instruments, they started to play. Uncle Joe's Band, Sy and Allison crowded into the sound room.

"I think it's Jane," Ian said quietly.

Sy looked at him. "Why?"

"She doesn't know her father."

Allison shook her head. "Wouldn't draw that conclusion too quickly. Lots of kids don't know their dad."

Ian nodded. "Agreed. I'll need to talk to the others."

Stygian Teal's first song started with a rhythmic drumbeat, followed by a short guitar solo, after which Jane began to melodically sing.

> *Ain't goin' to see the world, all black and blue*
> *Ain't goin' to see the world, or you know who*
> *Ain't goin' to see the world, you got the time*
> *Ain't goin' to see the world, you got yours and I got mine-*

With the first verse completed, Jane's voice darkened and dropped an octave.

> *I know you hate the blue sky*
> *There isn't a reason, look into my eye*
> *I know you hate the earth*
> *There isn't a reason, for what it's worth*
>
> *It's all we've got, the big blue spot*
> *Where we all live, it's not a lot*

After another verse and chorus Stygian Teal stopped and looked at the control booth. Sy clicked the intercom. "Very nice. Could work on the lyrics a bit, and you might add a bit more baseline, but not bad." Sara smiled and looked at Kara, who also grinned.

In the booth Rick whispered to Rod, "I think it was kind of dark."

Rod smirked. "Dude. We're a metal band. *We're* kind of dark."

"Oh yeah."

Stygian Teal's second song started with a long guitar riff. Sy asked that they play something a bit different from the first song and Jane announced they had an original folk song the group had been working on, so the guitar riff came as something of a surprise. The opening riff was followed by a drum interlude and the very gradual addition of the bass. It wasn't until several minutes after the song started that Jane began to sing.

> *This ain't no time for leaving, the time has come and gone*
> *You should remember everything you had when I'm singin'*
> *you this song*
>
> *I'm getting out of this lie, the hell that hath no fury*

No fury like mine now
No fury like mine now
No fury like mine now
I'm coming to find the time, you better find the how

Remember the times we saw each other at the school
Remember the times we went and broke the golden rule

This ain't no time for leaving, the time has come and gone
You should remember everything you had when I'm singin'
you this song

As Jane began to sing the chorus Sy held up her hand and the band stopped playing. "That's a pretty harsh sound for a folk song."

Sara nodded. "Yeah, Kara wrote it after she broke up with her boyfriend."

Sy looked at Rick. "Yup." She turned back to Stygian Teal. "What do you think about making it a little less folksy and a little more metallic?"

The band members looked at each other. Jane nodded toward the control room. "Um, sure. We could try that."

Sy waved her hand. "Okay, let's take a break." She turned toward Ian. "How about you guys play something?"

Ian smiled. "That would be lovely. Perhaps a bit of inspiration for the young ladies."

"Mostly I was thinking you need to practice."

As the two bands switched places Sy crossed her arms. Having worked with Sy for a few years, the members of Uncle Joe's Band knew when Sy had a plan. Her brow was furrowed and her lips pursed. Allison sidled next to her and without looking in her direction quietly mumbled, "Are you thinking what I think you're thinking?" to which Sy shot her a knowing glance.

The Stygian Teal band-mates avoided appearing overly impressed as Uncle Joe's Band rattled off a few of their more popular songs. Still, Indira couldn't help but smile broadly as Ian screamed out the lyrics of Broken Slipper, their first hit.

Don't need no prince, no castle too...
Don't need no dress, you wasted fool...
I'm my own fairy godmother...

I'll get my own ride, to the prince's ball
Keep your happy ending, I'll take the fall.

Break the glass slipper
Break the glass slipper

Don't need no prince, I'm made of stone
Keep your carriage, I walk alone
Go tell stepmother
She's a slave, she's a bitch...
I'm going to go now, scratch an itch...

Break the glass slipper
Break the glass slipper

As the song reached its end, Sy waved her hand. "Okay. You guys clearly need to practice." She turned to Kara. "They're going on tour and need some work."

"Where are they going?"

Sy sighed. "Asia. Mostly Japan. They're developing a following there and we want it to grow."

"Japan, I love Japan." Kara replied. "I love manga, sushi and Pokémon."

Jane smirked. "Pokémon?"

Kara put her hands on her hips. "Do we need to talk about your obsession with Totoro?"

Jane stopped smirking. "Totoro is a symbol of spiritual comfort and the healing power of nature."

Kara rolled her eyes. "I've seen the movie. Totoro is an overweight cat."

After a brief, awkward silence, Sy waved her hands. "Whatever the heck Totoro is, you all need to practice. I'm going to set up a schedule."

After Stygian Teal left, Sy waved Uncle Joe's Band into the living room for an impromptu meeting. As the bandmates sat, she stood, hands on her hips. "Okay, we're going to be touring Japan in a couple weeks. I've set up a practice schedule, an outline of dates, and so on. Now, we have a few things to decide. First, I need you to come up with a couple new songs between now and then. I know it's short notice, but it will be good to try them out before we start the recording process. Second, I've decided that Allison will be joining us. I'm officially making her a 'crew member.'"

Allison smiled. "I get to be a roadie! I can't wait to tell my friends."

Sy continued. "Finally, we need another opening act. Lead Paint backed out at the last minute. There's a Thai group that one of the label subsidiaries represents who might be able to fill the void on such short notice, but we need to decide if they'll work."

Steve raised his hand. "What about the group that was just here? Stiggy Till?"

Rod shook his head. "They're name is Steel Teal."

Rick coughed. "I thought it was Stylin' Tall."

Ian rolled his eyes. "Bloody hell. It's Stygian, S-T-Y-G-I-A-N, Teal, T-E-A-L. Stygian means from the river Styx, and Teal is a blue-green color. They're named for the color of the river Styx. It's bloody poetic."

The room was quiet for a moment. Rod broke the silence. "Oh right. That makes total sense. I just didn't hear it correctly."

Sy raised her hand. "Whatever their name, I'm not sure they're ready for an international tour. They're still a local group without much name recognition."

Rod smiled. "So were we. And here we are now."

Ian nodded. "Quite right. We needed a chance to break out. Pay it forward. I say."

"And it will give us a chance to figure out which one is Ian's kid," Rick added.

Sy turned to Allison. "What do you think?"

Allison crossed her arms. "I think it would be good. It will provide balance. An all-girl punk band opening for a metal band. It kind of works."

Sy sighed. "Okay then. I don't think they have a manager, so I'll talk to them directly. And they're going to have to practice." She paused. "A lot."

Ian stood. "It's settled then. We're touring with Stygian Teal."

Rod raised his hand. "What's the name of this tour?"

Sy smiled. "We're calling it the Shattered Unicorn Tour."

Rod nodded.

Shattered Unicorn was Uncle Joe's Band most recent release. Sy and the recording company had hoped it would lead to even greater fanfare than the group had experienced previously, catapulting Uncle Joe's Band into ever greater stardom. As with many heightened expectations, reality had proven far less satisfying. In response, Sy had suggested focusing on the international market, where, on occasion, domestic mediocrity can flourish.

Allison smirked. "You should call it the father-daughter tour."

Ian shot her a look. "If only we knew who the daughter was..."

CHAPTER 3

Jo Ojisan

Mystery Uncle
chases the sublime haiku
in the rising sun

—Jo Ojisan

At the same time Uncle Joe was traversing North America in his Volkswagen bus, Joji Kinsara wandered throughout the Japanese Archipelago in a Subaru Kei. Adorned on the sides with stickers from Mt Fuji, an Andy Warhol-like can of mushrooms, some Pokémon characters, and the sigil from the Sumiyoshi-kai, Joji's Subaru traversed the roads and byways of every prefecture, city, and village. Throughout his journeys he would frequently become intrigued by something, anything really, that spoke to his whimsical and spiritual musings. In those moments he would write, publicly, on something he hoped passersby would read. Always in white paint he always wrote in traditional haiku with great care to ensure his kanjis were selected to maintain whatever feeling had been elicited. And, as time progressed, his haikus grew in popular perception. Always signed simply ジョ (Jo), his work became an iconic part of the Japanese landscape.

Like Dansky or Atticus, the public never recognized Joji Kinsara as the poet known as Jo. The very enigmatic nature of Jo's person became part of the lore surrounding his poetry, such that whenever a new haiku was recognized, art critics, reporters, and cultural commentators would incessantly discuss what the great artist was trying to convey, who he or she might be, and when the painted kanjis had been scribed.

Not one to read a newspaper or magazine or observe any other sort of media, by the time of his death in the early 2000s, Joji Kinsara never realized how famous he had become. Books of his haikus were translated into dozens of languages. Photographs of his works were common in tourist shops and airports. Originals sold at auction for hundreds of thousands of dollars. Yet Joji remained oblivious to it all.

Thought by many to be an aged monk wandering on foot from village to village in the tradition of artists from bygone eras, the *idea* of "Jo" gradually became as important as the poetry itself. People imagined Jo as the oddball relative, one with a penchant for reading and writing, who showed up late for dinner with a strange new story or seemed lost to themselves until they blurted out a powerful bit of wisdom.

The real Jo was a far more modest figure than the public might imagine. Slight in stature, usually adorned in a T-shirt and sweatpants under a haori jacket, he made his way from place to place in an old Subaru van, often sleeping in the back of the van or on the ground nearby.

In time the idea that everyone knew "Jo" became so pervasive that the haiku master known as "Jo" took on a friendlier nom de guerre and became popularly known as Jo Ojisan, further reflecting the familial relationship many felt for the artist.

For the next few weeks Stygian Teal met at the loft for daily practice sessions. Sy asked that Uncle Joe's Band not distract from their efforts. Rick, Steve, Rod, and Ian made sure to avoid bursting into the studio, offering words of advice, or generally inserting themselves in the preparatory process Sy had suggested.

When it came time to start the tour, Uncle Joe's Band, Allison, and Sy made their way to the San Francisco Airport as a small mountain of equipment, encased in various crates and boxes, were loaded by half a dozen crew members onto a truck. The truck followed the band who, upon arriving at the airport, made their way to a large lounge off the main terminal where groups embarking on private planes waited to board. As a plane was loaded with their equipment the band sat and scrolled through their phones.

As an opening act that wasn't expected to provide much of a draw, Stygian Teal wasn't allowed to bring their own equipment, so Sy had suggested the all-female band simply meet Uncle Joe's entourage at the airport.

Allison, it was clear, hadn't fully interpreted what it meant to "be part of the crew." Whatever glamor she envisioned was erased as she helped to load the truck and then the plane. By the time the crew had finished she stumbled into the lounge, exhausted.

Rod patted the seat next to him on the couch. "My daughter's first summer job. You're doing great."

Allison flopped down next to him. "I can't believe I signed up for this."

Steve smiled. "The point of summer jobs with hard physical work is to learn that you don't want to do them when you get older."

"I've learned. I'd like to stop now."

Rod put his arm around her. "I wouldn't want to deprive you of the full experience."

Sy, who had been talking on her phone, suddenly looked up. "Where is Stygian Teal?"

Ian stood up and looked around the lounge, which was sparsely populated with a few clusters of business travelers and the members of a basketball team. "Bloody hell. We can't take off without them."

Sy motioned to Uncle Joe's Band. "We have to find them. The plane is scheduled to take off in a few minutes." She tapped her phone and held it up to her ear. After a moment she turned to the group. "No answer. They're probably in the main terminal somewhere. Let's split up and see if we can find them."

Rick, Rod, and Steve, ready to do something other than stare at their phones, jumped to their feet and followed Ian and Sy into the crowded main terminal.

Steve was the first to spot the Stygian Teal band members, crowded around a pair of ticket agents at a United Airlines desk. Jane appeared to be loudly talking to the agents while Kara, Indira, and Sara stood with their arms folded, looking very annoyed.

"We just want to know what our flight number is," Jane said, with a look of exasperation on her face.

One of the agents, stone-faced, responded. "Ma'am, we don't know what flight you are on. It should be on your ticket."

"I don't have a ticket."

"Then maybe you aren't on a flight."

"I would be if I knew the flight number!"

"Look, lady, you're going to have to go to the counter, wait in line like everyone else, and tell them your name to figure out what flight you're on."

Jane pointed at the counter. "That line is huge! We'll miss our flight."

The agent grumbled, "How do you know? You don't even know what flight you're on."

"And thanks to your complete incompetence and inability to provide even the most basic information, we'll probably never find out!"

The agent's inexpressive face began to appear annoyed. "That's it. I'm calling security." She reached for the walkie talkie attached to her belt.

"Wait, wait, wait..." Steve quickly ran up to the group and put his hand on the agent's arm. "It's okay, no need for security." He turned to Jane. "Miss Eilish, we've got your plane ready."

Kara raised her eyebrows. Steve shot her a wink. She smiled. "I wondered where you were! Dozens of Billie Eilish fans are going to be disappointed if we don't get on that plane."

The agents looked confused.

Steve continued. "Yes, your plane is right this way."

One of the agents frowned. "She doesn't look like Billie Eilish."

Kara waved her hand. "Of course not. She just had her hair redone." She lowered her voice to a whisper. "I mean, how could she go out in public without being recognized if she still looked, well, like Billie Eilish?"

The other agent nodded. "Yeah, that makes sense."

Steve took Jane's arm. "Right this way."

"Wait!" One of the agents held up a hand. "Can we get a picture?"

Jane looked at Steve. "Um, sure. Of course."

The agent held up her phone to take a selfie and Jane leaned in. "Great, now we really have to go." Steve insisted.

Indira rolled her eyes. "Yeah. *Miss Eilish* can't wait for her plane."

Steve took Jane's arm and began marching toward the lounge.

Joji Kinsara was in his mid-teens when his family traveled from

Sapporo to Honolulu in the summer of 1970. During that auspicious trip Joji changed. For years his family tried to imagine what it was that had happened during their visit to the island state that triggered his metamorphosis. After the trip it was clear Joji had discovered something spiritual and imaginative deep within his soul. After his return home he became introspective and observative. Despite great speculation his family never understood what occurred during that auspicious trip, or why.

Even before the trip to Honolulu there had been hints Joji was different. A precocious and independent youth, Joji had managed to evade his parents' desires to pursue advanced schooling, a responsible apprenticeship, or any activity that might result in a stable career. Though never disrespectful, Joji often seemed lost in his own head, such that teachers and mentors were left to rap his knuckles or pinch his ears to ensure he was paying attention.

By the time Joji returned from their family trip, his parents had largely given up pushing him toward a career. His twin sister, Juri, who was far more successful and ambitious, had become the focus of their attention. While Juri stayed long hours after reading, writing, and preparing for a future in business or industry, Joji would sit alone in his room, staring at a butterfly or a flower. Efforts to "encourage" his progress were largely futile.

Joji's father, vice president of a company that produced soft drinks and beer, tried to secure an apprenticeship for his son with his company's brewmaster. Days after the apprenticeship had begun the brewmaster stormed into the vice president's office, sat a glass of beer in front of him and pointedly demanded that he taste it. Joji's father took a swig and promptly spit it out across his desk and onto the brewmaster. After some tortured conversation he learned that over five thousand gallons of the company's finest ale had been contaminated.

When Joji's career as a brewmaster failed, his father sought to have him placed with a well-known master knifemaker in hopes he might learn the trade. After that he was sent to become a Buddhist monk, only to be kicked out of the monastery for falling asleep while meditating.

Finally, out of desperation, Joji's parents simply gave him the keys to the Subaru Kei van and told him he would have to find his way on his own.

The flight from San Francisco International Airport to Tokyo took twelve hours, owing to minimal headwinds and the pilot's desire to arrive early enough to attend a friend's birthday dinner. Uncle Joe's Band had learned that the key to travel, to performing on the road, was less the effect of careful preparation than that of sleep. Time zones, odd hours, strange venues were all manageable if the performer simply slept through as much of the tour as was feasible. Thus, Uncle Joe's Band spent most of the flight to Tokyo reclined in their seats, window shades down fast asleep.

In contrast, Stygian Teal's excitement made sleep a near impossibility. They sat as a group near the rear of the plane watching movies, playing on their phones, and trying to look as unenthused as possible while on a private plane flying to a distant airport to begin their first tour outside the San Francisco Bay area. Sy had advised the group to try and get as much rest as possible, but to no avail.

Allison sat near the back of the plane with the girl band, tired from loading the truck and plane, but nearly as excited as the band members. For her first trip outside the United States she had made careful preparation, learning as much about the culture and language of Japan as was feasible within a few weeks.

As the plane crossed the 180th Meridian, Sara made her way back from the restroom and plopped down next to Allison, who was practicing her Japanese on a Duolingo app.

"Can I ask you a question?" Sara asked.

Allison took off her headset. "Of course."

"How does it feel to have a dad who's a rock star?"

Allison smiled. "I didn't know him until a few years ago. Back then he wasn't much of a rock star. Honestly, I'm not sure he is now."

"You didn't know your dad growing up?"

Allison shook her head.

Sara sighed. "Neither did I. My mom didn't say much about him either, which just made it worse."

After a moment of silence, Allison asked, "Did you ever want to know who he was?"

"Yes and no. I have fantasies about him, who he is and what he does. I think if I ever really found out I'd probably be disappointed.

What happened when you found out about your dad?"

Allison thought for a moment. "It was different than I expected. I had the same ideas about my dad. I thought he'd be some kind of really charming, charismatic guy that didn't stay with my mom because he had some important job or something. He wasn't really any of those things. But, somehow getting to know him has been better. He didn't leave my mom or run away from me or anything like that. I was afraid he had run away and didn't want me or didn't want to be a part of my life, but it turns out he just didn't know. Which is totally different than I expected."

Sara tapped the seat rest. "I never knew my dad. My mom said the same thing, that he walked out when I was little. I don't even remember him. I get what you mean about thinking he's someone important, but every time I think about him, I get angry, which doesn't really make sense because I don't know whether he even knows about me. My mom is kind of off sometimes."

"When did you decide to join a band?" Allison asked.

Sara smiled. "Jane and I met in high school. We didn't fit in with most of the other girls. We were in the marching band."

Allison laughed. "You were in the marching band?"

"We even went to band camp one summer."

"What instrument did Jane play?"

Sara looked sideways and whispered, "The trombone."

Allison giggled.

"She was actually really good."

"When did you start Stygian Teal?"

"It was after one of the band directors made a pass at her."

Allison's eyes got big. "Really? That's terrible. What happened?"

Sara smirked. "I don't really know, exactly. We were in class one day, getting ready to start, you know, warming up. Somehow, she ended up alone with him in the storage closet. There was this loud crash and a yell and she came storming out with her trombone all bent out of shape. She was yelling, seriously pissed. Then a minute later he comes out limping with a gash over his eye. He tells her to go to the office and she flips him off and throws her trombone at him. Hit him in the stomach. Hard. Best throw I've ever seen."

"What happened to Jane?"

"Obviously she didn't go back to band class. The school was going to expel her until they found out he'd tried to grope her. She threatened to sue and they acted like nothing happened. And, of course, the band director went on leave."

Allison looked across the aisle. Jane was watching a movie on the small screen in front of her. "That would be devastating."

"After she left the school band, Jane turned dark for a time. She started wearing all this goth stuff and started listening to punk and metal. Then one day out of nowhere she comes up to me and asks if I can play the drums for real. I told her I could and she invited me to play in a band she was putting together. That's when I met Kara and Indira.

"At first our music was bad. Really dark and kind of boring. I think Jane was working through her issues and the music kind of helped her do that. Over time we started expanding a bit and it got better and better. As her issues got better, so did the music."

Allison nodded. "I think that's what happened to my dad's band. They weren't very good and then suddenly they got better."

"Maybe they had issues to work through too."

"Maybe."

Sara looked at Jane, who was still watching the screen on the seat in front of her. "OMG. She's watching *Totoro* again."

"*Totoro*?"

Sara rolled her eyes. "It's this Japanese movie about a girl and a giant spirit cat. Jane is *obsessed*."

The plane touched down at Tokyo International Airport early in the evening. The two bands made their way through the concourse, where they stopped in a VIP lounge awaiting a bus to their hotel. As they waited, Rick sauntered off to find a restroom. When he returned, he had a look of transcendental bliss on his face.

"What happened to you?" Rod asked.

"I have just had the most wonderful experience," Rick said as he flopped down on one of the couches in the lounge.

"What happened?"

"I went to the bathroom," Rick said without a hint of irony.

Steve rolled his eyes. "Yeah. Okay."

"You don't understand. I'm serious. It was amazing."

Indira set down her backpack. "Well, I have to go, so maybe I'll have an amazing experience, too."

Several minutes later Indira returned with a similarly blissful look on her face. "He's right. It's amazing."

Rick nodded at Indira. "See."

Ian pulled his sunglasses down his nose. "What the bloody hell are you two talking about? It's a bathroom, with a toilet. You do your business."

Sy, who had been texting on her phone while the others talked, looked up. "It's the toilets. Everybody loves Japanese toilets when they try them for the first time."

Ian's brow furrowed. "What's so great about Japanese toilets?"

Rick pointed in the direction of the restroom. "The Japanese have perfected the art of going to the bathroom. Their toilets are so sophisticated they come with a control panel. An *actual* control panel."

Steve scratched his arm. "What does it control?"

"Everything. You sit down and there are arm-rests with lots of buttons on them. Push a button and the seat warms up. You push another button, music comes on. Push another and a video game pad appears. There's one that squirts water up to clean you off and another that blows air to dry you afterwards."

Indira chimed in. "I think I pushed one that activated a back massage."

Steve raised a skeptical eyebrow. "Japanese toilets can do all that?"

"And more. There were a whole bunch of other buttons I didn't even try. I'm going to wait until I have to go again and then try some more," Rick replied.

Sara stood. "I think I have to go." She started walking toward the bathroom. Kara, Jane, and Allison quickly followed.

Sy grimaced. "Jesus, the bus will be here any minute. Maybe we can all go before it gets here." She looked at Ian, Steve, and Rob. "You know there's a whole country full of Japanese toilets. It's called Japan."

"Yup, and we might need to try them all," Rod replied as he followed the girls.

CHAPTER 4

Mt. Fuji

The lake hand rises
Points to the sacred mountain
Gathering its tears

—Jo Ojisan

Late in the summer of 1972, Joji found himself camping in the Aokigahara Forest near Mount Fuji. The forest was a famed venue for stories of ghosts, demons, and magical creatures. Ever interested in nature and magic, Jo parked his van in an open area near a lake with a stunning view of Mt. Fuji, made himself a bowl of ramen, and sat on a mat to watch the sunset. It was summer and the air was warm. He watched as the fireflies swarmed above the lake and the reddened sky gradually grew dark. Slowly his eyelids drooped and he fell into a blissful sleep.

Around two o'clock in the morning Joji woke. The moon was nearly full and lit up the snow on the cap of the mountain. Rays of moonlight bounced off the limbs of trees and illuminated the waters of the lake. In the water the strange glow of bioluminescence followed fish and frogs that moved beneath the surface.

Joji stood and walked a few steps toward the lake, inspired by his serene surroundings. As he peered into the lake, he saw what appeared to be a giant arm, a few feet from the shore, reaching toward the surface. The arm waved back and forth in the water as though some ethereal creature was letting the water run through its fingers as it stretched to escape its watery abode.

For a few moments Joji watched, enthralled, wondering how the combination of moonlight and detritus in the lake had managed to create such a surreal impression. Then, as if to answer, the hand attached to the arm pierced the surface of the lake, causing a small ripple that made its way to shore.

Joji was terrified. He stepped away from the edge of the lake fearful of whatever the hand might be attached to. The hand bobbed up and down a bit, its fingers and knuckles fixed, so that eventually an elbow emerged and then a bit of shoulder. The arm floated in the serene lake for several minutes.

Curiosity gradually replaced Joji's terror and he found a long stick on the shore that could reach the floating arm. Ever so gently he reached out and touched the hand with the stick. It didn't move. He poked it. The hand and attached arm dove beneath the surface before bobbing back to the top once again. Joji stretched out further, wedging the stick between two of the fingers and pulling the arm to shore.

The hand and arm were perfectly formed and did not move. Joji sat by them for a moment before touching one of the fingers. It was cold and didn't budge. He touched the hand and marveled at the smoothness of the skin. He tapped it and was surprised when it sounded hollow. He turned it over and picked it up. It was lighter than he expected. Where the shoulder was supposed to attach to the thorax there was the metal clasp. It wasn't until he saw the kanji's next to the clasp, barely visible in the moonlight that he realized the arm belonged to Shiro's Department Store.

———————

The next morning Joji waded out into the shallow waters near his van. He left the arm sitting on shore, with the shoulder stuck in the ground so that it appeared the hand was pointing at the lake. In the shallow water he found a bicycle tire, part of a refrigerator, rusting car parts, and some algae covered clothes, which he pulled from the water and dragged to shore. As he waded further, he pulled more and more junk from the lake and set them in a pile. For several hours he waded and piled. By evening the pile of garbage that he had exhumed from the lake towered above his head. As evening came the shadow of Mt. Fuji fell across the lake and onto the garbage pile. Joji looked at the shadow. He looked at the pile of garbage. As the sun set, he began reorganizing the pile, moving a dilapidated car seat here, a rusting fencepost there. When he finished the silhouette of the garbage pile matched the silhouette of Mt. Fuji.

The next day Joji walked around his garbage Mt. Fuji. As he stepped over a broken easel, he tripped on a paint can. He noticed the can was full and unopened. After digging through some of the other items in the trash pile he found an opener and a brush.

It is unclear what happens during any given moment of artistic inspiration. For some it may be their environment that lights the spark of creativity. For others a fleeting thought or hint of imagination rising from the depths of conjecture. And for others the rekindling of a memory; a plaintive thought or a shard of an old idea stirs the energies that give rise to artistic expression.

Whatever the cause, the paint can, mound of garbage and distant vista of Mt. Fuji came together in Joji's mind. He stood a few feet away from the pile near the thick trunk of a red cedar and opened the paint can lid. With a flick of his wrist, he sunk the brush into the paint before lifting it to the tree. On the tree trunk he painted several kanjis in a quick flourish.

Kenji Tanaka took his camera everywhere. Five years working at the *Tokyo Shimbun* (newspaper) had left him with enough missed opportunities to realize that cataloging the events that make up the news had less to do with finding out what might happen than being prepared when something did. Disasters, celebrations, and scandals can catch even the most ardent reporter unaware. Thus, having tools of the trade on hand at all times had become Kenji's habit.

On a midsummer afternoon Kenji returned from reporting on a factory shutdown southeast of Tokyo. He drove his Toyota van in a circuitous route, snaking his way along a group of back-roads, stopping to take pictures of the small villages along the way.

As Kenji made his way around a lake, he saw Mt. Fuji and considered stopping to take a few pictures of the mountain for future use. In a remote area near the lakeshore, he pulled off the road and parked his car. While walking through the trees he looked for a vista that might include the mountain and lake. As he pushed through a small grove, he happened upon Joji's pile of garbage.

After several minutes of trying to discern the garbage's origins, the young reporter noticed Joji's haiku painted next to the garbage pile. His eyes grew as he began to consider the meaning imposed by the words. He checked his pockets to ensure he had enough film.

Three days later Joji's haiku, painted on the tree next to the pile of garbage perfectly shaped like Mt. Fuji set against a backdrop of the great mountain itself was plastered across the front page of *Tokyo Shimbun*. The headline read, "The Garbage on the Mountain" and was followed by a story about the waste that had been allowed to collect on and around Mt. Fuji.

Two weeks later the members of the Japanese Diet held up copies of the *Tokyo Shimbun* with Kenji's photograph of Joji's haiku and loudly proclaimed the need to preserve a national treasure. Bills were passed, committees investigated, and agencies were created to ensure that Japan would clean up and never spoil its great places again.

When the bands finally reached the hotel in downtown Tokyo, Stygian Teal was exhausted. Unlike the members of Uncle Joe's Band, who were careful to ensure they got as much sleep as possible, the women had stayed awake for most of the flight and appeared nearly incoherent when they arrived. After checking in, Sy directed Stygian Teal to their rooms and ordered some food to be delivered.

While Stygian Teal were being sent to their rooms, Uncle Joe's Band made their way to a small restaurant across the street from the hotel. Sitting together at a small table next to the street they ordered a variety of sushi dishes. As they did, the waiter set the table for them, with chopsticks and several small dishes and plates.

Steve pulled apart his chopsticks and began to arrange the little bowls and dishes. He pointed at a small rectangular bowl. "What's this one?"

Rick rolled his eyes. "Duh, it's for the soy sauce."

"Oh." Steve reached across the table for the small ceramic bottle of soy sauce and poured it into the dish. As he did, the waiter returned to the table.

The waiter pointed at the dish and waved his hands. "No."

Steve looked at Rick. "I thought you said it was for the soy sauce."

"I thought it was."

Steve nodded at the waiter. "It's okay. It may be the wrong dish, but I'll make it work."

The waiter shook his head, "no" and started to reach for the dish.

Ian held up his hand. "It's all right, mate. He'll just use the dish he's already put the sauce in. It'll be fine."

The waiter shook his head, sighed, and wandered back to the kitchen.

A few minutes later the waiter returned with several plates of sushi and miso soup. He set them down on the table and tried to put a small dish next to Steve and take away the not-for-soy-sauce dish Steve had inadvertently filled with the dark, salty liquid.

Steve held up his hand. "Dude. It's fine."

The waiter turned and marched back toward the kitchen, muttering.

As the bandmates dug into the sushi the waiter returned, this time with one of the chefs from the kitchen. The chef pointed to the dish and shook his head. "Is bad."

Steve grimaced. "The dish is fine. I'm using it for my sushi. Thank you very much for your concern."

The waiter shrugged and said something in Japanese to the chef, who, appearing confounded, replied. After a few moments of back and forth, both turned away from the table and marched back to the kitchen.

After the waiter and chef left, Uncle Joe's Band ate in silence for several minutes. The silence was interrupted when Rod noticed a man in a green jacket standing on the street outside the window pointing at Steve.

"What's he on about?" Ian asked.

The man in the green jacket waved at Steve and moved his hands back and forth while shaking his head. Steve picked up a piece of sushi, smiled at the man, dipped it in his soy sauce, and put it in his mouth. He gave the man a thumbs-up.

The man in the green jacket shook his head, threw up his hands, and walked away.

The band ate their way through several sushi rolls by the time

Allison crossed the street and sat down at the table.

Rick patted his abdomen. "You've got to try the one with the salmon and cucumbers. It's divine."

Rod handed her a menu. She scanned the menu and put it down. "It looks great. I can't wait to post on my Instagram that I'm having sushi in Japan." She looked at the remaining pieces on the plates around the table. After a moment her eyes fell on Steve's soy sauce dish. "Steve." She pointed at the dish. "Why are you using an ashtray for your soy sauce?"

CHAPTER 5

Tokyo

In the land of the rising sun
I sing on stage when the moon goes dark
And the light of the spotlight
Means there's a song to be sung

—Uncle Joe's Band, "Somewhere on Stage"

When the bus dropped off Uncle Joe's Band and Stygian Teal in front of the auditorium, the musicians looked up at the marquee, which read in Japanese (and English) "Uncle Joe's Band Live w. Stygian Teal." The members of Stygian Teal looked at the marquee out of sheer amazement and delight, while the members of Uncle Joe's Band looked to ensure they had been dropped off at the correct venue.

A year prior, in Paris, Uncle Joe's Band found themselves in front of a football stadium after a bus driver had inadvertently assumed the band was a group of German soccer enthusiasts in town to watch Paris Saint-Germain play Bayern Munich in a Champions League match. Many of the Paris Saint-Germain fans apparently assumed the group was German as well. As the band tried to make their way to the stadium's entrance they were pelted with all manner of leftover food, beer bottles, and cups. It wasn't until they reached the inner gate that they realized this wasn't a rock concert and the people cursing at them weren't fans simply expressing their inner metalhead. After that experience the members of Uncle Joe's Band always read the marquee to ensure they were in the right venue.

The auditorium in Tokyo was an older building, at one time a place where concert goers might have expected to see an orchestra or ballet. Recently refurbished, it had been converted into something more industrial, with concrete platforms and an open ceiling where pipes and electrical wires could be seen. The sides of the auditorium were painted with giant anime rock band characters, guitars, and microphones.

Stygian Teal stopped outside the doors of the auditorium and stared at the giant characters. Allison took several pictures of the girl band and a short video for their rapidly growing social media following. In the pictures and video, the Stygian Teal band members appeared nonchalant and aloof. Off camera they were effusive and excited.

As the two bands entered the arena Sy pointed each to their dressing rooms. Allison headed to the stage to help the crew set up for the show. A half hour later Sy called Stygian Teal to the stage for a sound check. After they made their way to the stage Sy called them into a huddle. "Okay. This isn't like playing in a club. The space is much much larger so you're going to have to get loud. Be as loud as you possibly can."

Jane and the other band members nodded.

Sy stepped off the stage out into the auditorium and the band started to play. Several times she raised her hands to encourage more sound.

When they had finished Jane shook her head. "I'm going to be hoarse when this is over."

Sy nodded. "Welcome to the big time. Now tonight you are going to have to be at *least* that loud. There will be thousands of people in here, which will further dampen the sound." She looked each band member in the eye. "So be *loud.*"

Jane whispered to Sara, "I'll bet the guys have trouble making this much noise every night."

Sy overheard the whisper. She looked at Jane and pointed to the rear of the auditorium. "Go sit in the back and listen."

Stygian Teal had taken their seats near the back of the auditorium when Uncle Joe's Band started to play. They could nearly feel the sound of the guitar chords as they resonated off the walls. Kara covered her ears. Jane fell out of her seat.

Sara looked at the others. "How do they do that?"

Indira shook her head. "What did you say?"

Sara replied, nearly shouting, "How do they do that?"

Jane got up off the floor. "How indeed?" She looked toward the sound control room sitting behind the last row. "They want us to sing until we lose our voice and then they turn up the volume for them." Her face reddened and she marched around the seats and knocked on the sound room door.

The door opened and a head popped out. "Oh hey. What can we do for you?"

Jane grimaced. "Did you guys change the settings from our sound check to theirs?"

The head nodded. "Heck yes. Why do you ask?"

"You turned up the amplification when the male band played and kept it lower when we played." She cocked her head and put her hands on her hips.

The eyes on the head blinked. "No. Of course not."

"Really. You just said you changed the settings."

The eyes on the head blinked again. "Yeah, we changed the settings. We turned them down." The head nodded toward the stage. "They're way too loud to use the same amplification as you."

Jane's hands dropped to her sides. "Oh."

"Is there anything else I can help you with?"

Jane shook her head and walked back to the group.

After the sound check both bands walked back to the dressing rooms and waited for the evening's show.

After she finished helping to set up the stage Allison walked into Stygian Teal's dressing room. The band members were sitting on a pair of couches across from each other, heads down, humming together. She stood in a corner and waited until Sara picked up her head and motioned for her to sit with the group.

"This is how we get ready for a show," Sara said.

Allison, alternately aware that every performer prepares for a concert differently and sitting in a group humming seemed a rather odd way to do so, replied, "Okay."

Several minutes of humming later, Jane stopped, took a deep breath, and stood up. "I think we're ready," she said with an air of certainty.

"Damn right we're ready," Indira replied.

"We have our song list; we've practiced and we're ready to blow their freaking minds," Kara said as she stood.

Allison smiled. "Awesome. You guys sound totally primed." She stood up next to Jane. "Out of curiosity are you going to introduce yourself in Japanese or English?"

A look of panic swept across the faces of Stygian Teal. Jane started to hyperventilate. "Oh crap! I didn't think of that. What are we going to say? I mean I can't say anything in Japanese. I'll probably say something wrong. I'll call the audience a bunch of ugly pigeons. They're going to get mad. We'll get thrown out of the country!"

Kara sat back down as though her entire body had deflated.

Indira started to tear up.

Allison held up her hands. "It's okay. It's okay. We'll totally get you ready. You only have to remember a few words in Japanese. You'll be fine. You can even write them down and I'll tape them to the stage floor."

Jane put her hands on the sides of her face. "You. don't understand. I don't remember anything on stage. Singing is like muscle memory for me. I'll totally freeze up. Or say something wrong. This isn't like singing."

"Maybe someone else can introduce the band."

Indira and Sara shook their heads. Kara looked panicked. "We don't ever try to speak on stage. Ever. We'll do some backup vocal stuff, but nothing impromptu."

Jane began to pace. "Maybe we can just sing and not tell them who we are. I mean, they know who we are anyway, right? Maybe we just pretend like we're there playing some songs and the audience just happens to be there and it's just a big coincidence and they don't really care."

Allison sat back on the couch. "This is your first major concert and you're not going to introduce yourselves. To a totally new market. Full of totally new people." She shot Jane a skeptical look. "Please."

Indira crossed her arms. "We can't go down like this. We worked way too hard to have our big break blown because we're afraid to say something to our fans."

Kara looked at Allison. "You introduce us."

Allison raised her eyebrows. "Me? I'm not part of the band. And

I don't speak Japanese."

Sara nodded. "Yes. Yes, you could be. Or you don't have to be. You just come out and introduce us. That's all you have to do. Tell people who we are. Just a few words in Japanese. You can memorize them or write them down."

Indira touched Allison's arm. "Please. Please do this. We need this."

Allison looked at the group. She stood up, this time turning toward the door. "I mean, I guess. I could come up with a few words, not many, mind you, just a few words about you guys."

Jane stopped pacing and put her hands on Allison's shoulders. "That's perfect. Just a few words. Nothing fancy. Just who we are and that we're happy to be here. Please."

Allison nodded. "Okay. I'd better go work on my Japanese." As she turned toward the door the members of Stygian Teal each gave her a hug.

When the show started, Sy was surprised when Allison led the girl band onto the stage. She was even more surprised when Allison began to speak to the crowd. "Rokku suru junbi wa dekite imasu ka? Stygian Teal no rokkunrōru ni sonaemashou." Allison pointed at the left side of the auditorium, "Kikoemasen" (*I can't hear you*), she said and raised her hand to her ear. She turned to the right side of the audience and did the same. As she turned to leave the stage the crowd caught a glimpse of the back of her leather jacket. In silver studs an outline of Hello Kitty raised her fist in a show of Kitty power. The crowd roared.

When Stygian Teal ended their performance and exited the stage, they appeared to the crew to be more excited than the crowd. High-fives and elated oh-my-God-can-you-believe-we-just-did-that were punctuated by the occasional high-pitched shriek. Sy pointed them toward their dressing room as the crew began to change over the stage for Uncle Joe's Band's performance.

"I can't believe we just did that!" Indira yelled.

Sara flopped down on one of the couches. "I know. That was *awesome*."

The door opened and Sy's head appeared. "Great job. Now come watch the rest of the show." She motioned back toward the stage. "And pay attention. Learn."

The members of Stygian Teal watched from offstage, as Uncle Joe's Band began its performance. As the room darkened Rod began a lengthy guitar riff punctuated by the intermittent sound of Steve's snare and bass drums. As the sound grew the bass guitar became audible. When the combined sound reached its deafening peak, it suddenly stopped, the auditorium lights came on, and Ian let out a piercing scream. The crowd roared.

Uncle Joe's Band played several songs. Each song differed from the next, each with its own tagline, hook, and rhythm. The lighting and effects changed with each song as well, such that some were played in near darkness and others with audience blinding back lighting. The Stygian Teal bandmates had been to plenty of concerts with other bands, but never watched as closely or carefully. Their elation turned to interest; each considered what she might do during the next performance to be a bit more like the band onstage.

CHAPTER 6

Godzilla

Wrecked urban center
Arrival, helping mobsters
Give the perfect gift

—Jo Ojisan

On January 17, 1995, the great Hanshin earthquake rocked Kobe, Japan. Within a matter of minutes thousands were killed and injured. Tens of thousands of buildings were destroyed and over a hundred thousand people were displaced.

One of the first rounds of relief provided in response to the disaster didn't come from Tokyo, the international community, or even the Japanese government, but from a large warehouse run by the Yakuza, the Japanese mafia, in the middle of the devastation. And a slight young man driving a Subaru van.

Joji woke to the sounds of someone tapping on the window of his van. The man standing outside was wearing a suit and tie, which seemed odd given the midnight hour. Joji sat up, rubbed his eyes, and rolled down his window.

"Good morning," the man said, without a hint of irony.

"I think it's still night," Joji replied.

"For you it is morning."

Joji opened his eyes wide to focus on the man. "If it's morning, I'm going back to sleep until noon."

"Nope. It's morning and time for you to move." The man looked slightly irritated.

"Why do I need to move?" Joji asked, wondering why in an unoccupied warehouse district in Kobe, anyone would care where he parked his van.

"Because your van is on private property," the man replied.

"Doesn't the government own the street?" Joji asked.

"Not this one."

"Who owns this street?"

"The Sumiyoshi-kai," the man said, lowering the sound of his voice and emphasizing "Sumiyoshi."

"What is Sumiyoshi?"

"Here, it is the government," the man said, offering no further explanation. "And if you do not move, things will not go well for you."

Joji opened his eyes wider. "In that case I'll move." He turned on the van.

Without a word the man in the suit turned and began to walk away.

"Wait," Joji said. "Does the Sumiyoshi government have an office where I can go to appeal for a permit to park?"

The man in the suit turned back and reached inside his suit. He pulled out a business card and handed it to Joji. "Now go," he said as he turned and walked away.

Joji drove his van to a different part of the city, closed his eyes and went to sleep. When he awoke, he looked at the business card. The card simply said "Sumiyoshi-Kai" and listed an address in downtown Kobe.

When Joji arrived at the address he found a large high-rise office building. In the lobby a security guard looked at the card and directed Joji to the eighth floor.

The Sumiyoshi-Kai's office looked like all the other accounting and law offices on the same floor. Large glass doors embossed with the Sumiyoshi name opened into a carpeted waiting room with clean white walls and a sitting area complete with a coffee table and dated magazines. Seated behind a reception desk was a secretary with a white blouse and blue skirt. She stood as Joji entered the room.

"Hello sir. How may I help you?" she asked with a bright smile.

"I'm looking for a place to park my van," Joji said. "I parked it last night but was told I had to move it because it was on a Sumiyoshi-kai street."

"Oh, you must have been near the port," the woman replied, her smile remaining unchanged. "That's where we control most of the streets."

"I like it there. It's much quieter than many other neighborhoods."

The woman picked up a clipboard and opened a filing cabinet. She clipped a form to the clipboard and handed it to Joji with a pen. "Fill this out and I'll see if one of our associates can meet with you."

Joji filled out the form, which asked for information about his family, what assets he owned and whether he belonged to any other organizations. He handed it back to the young woman, who motioned for him to wait.

After several minutes she escorted Joji down a hallway to a large office. Inside, a man wearing a blue suit and black tie sat behind a large mahogany desk. Joji could see tattoos across his hands and up both sides of his neck. He motioned for Joji to sit across the desk from him.

The man cleared his throat. "I understand you wish to park your van on our street."

Joji nodded.

"Our organization doesn't tolerate spies." The man's eyes narrowed. "We deal with them in ways they do not like."

"I am not a spy. I just want a quiet place to park my van," Joji replied.

The man tapped his fingers on the desk. "There are lots of quiet places in the city to park your van. You don't need to park by the port."

"I parked there because there was no one there at night."

"Well, there are lots of people there at night. Unless you are willing to pay, you can't park there."

Joji pulled out the pockets in his jacket. "I don't have any money to pay to park."

"Well, then you'll just have to go somewhere else," the man replied with an air of certainty.

Joji sighed. He stood and began to walk toward the door.

"Unless…" The man leaned back in his chair. "Unless you are willing to do something for me. For us."

Joji turned. "What do you want me to do?"

The man started tapping his fingers on the desk again. "We need some help moving things around in the warehouse." He paused. When Joji didn't respond he added, "We might even pay you for your work."

Joji, who was used to working odd jobs for a few yen, bowed. "I will work in the warehouse. Thank you for the job."

The man grunted and tapped his fingers on the desk. He handed Joji a piece of paper with an address.

———————

When the show ended and Uncle Joe's Band had exited the stage, both bands retreated to their dressing rooms. Allison helped the crew as it began the process of taking down the stage, and Sy talked on her phone, making sure the logistics were being prepared for the next show.

After Allison finished working with the crew, she retreated to a large greenroom in the back of the auditorium. The room had a high ceiling and concrete floor and was furnished with folding tables and chairs. Several movie posters hung on the walls. Seated around one of the tables were the members of Stygian Teal, Ian, and Rod. Jane had a notebook and pen. Ian was leaning back in his chair with his feet on the table. Rod looked bored.

"It's a process that requires self-actualization, but only in the sense that one actually is oneself," Ian said with a professorial air.

Jane looked confused. "So how do you actually write the lyrics?"

"It all has to flow from somewhere deep in the id, outside the realm of the superego and with a deep sense of unconscious assimilation."

Allison crossed her arms and looked at Jane. "Are you asking how he comes up with lyrics? Because it's pretty much none of that."

Ian pulled his sunglasses down his nose. "I beg your pardon."

Allison pulled up a chair and sat at the table. "It's simple really. Start with something you know. A concept. The color of the sun. How you feel about dogs. Alien abductions. Doesn't matter, just pick something. Then write lyrics describing what it means to you. Why it matters. Put it in words." She looked at Ian. "That's how *you* write your songs."

Ian pushed his sunglasses back up his nose. "Precisely. That's what I've been trying to tell them."

Jane put down her pen. "How do we start, you know, writing?"

Allison looked around the room. She pointed at a movie poster. "Start with that."

Jane stared intently at the poster. The words were all in Japanese, but the picture depicted Godzilla standing over a multi-headed dragon. Godzilla had one of the dragon heads in his arms and another was spewing flames.

"Write a song about Godzilla?" Jane asked skeptically.

"Start with Godzilla. What does Godzilla represent?" Allison asked.

"Fire and fury," Ian replied.

Allison turned toward Jane. "Okay, what else?"

"I don't know. Destruction? Power?"

Allison nodded. "Those are all correct. But what Godzilla really represents is even bigger. Godzilla is a metaphor for the Japanese. This country is plagued by disasters, earthquakes, tsunamis, and wars. Hiroshima and Nagasaki sit deep in the Japanese psyche. Godzilla is a metaphor for all those things. It's both a symbol of what has happened, what might happen, and hope that it will never happen again. It's a symbol of strength in the face of disaster."

"Uh, right. Of course. Disaster and resilience. Exactly what I meant." Ian nodded.

The members of Stygian Teal sat in amazement. Jane shook her head. "That's a lot to process."

Indira sat back in her chair. "Staring into Godzilla's eyes."

Sara smiled. "Godzilla's eyes." I think that's the title.

Jane started to write. "In Godzilla's eyes I've seen. The whole world pretty and green."

Kara looked at the poster. "I like the juxtaposition. Pretty green world and the fire of Godzilla."

Indira stood up, "The eyes of the monster burning it down, I see in those eyes the monster is me."

The room grew quiet. Indira cleared her throat. "Godzilla is a symbol of the catastrophe of global warming."

Allison nodded. "Yeah, we get it. Pretty good idea."

Ian sat up. "Yeah, kind of turns the whole metaphor thing on its head, doesn't it? Sort of like an inverted metaphor."

Sara's face looked confused. "What's an inverted metaphor?"

Ian put his hands together. "Wonderful question. In the paradigm of language an inverted metaphor is a metaphor that's been turned inside out. So, the part of the metaphor that was once in the middle is now on the outside, right there for everyone to see."

Allison smirked. "Yeah. That's what inverted means."

Ian continued to speak as though Allison hadn't said anything. "You see, the goal of the inverted metaphor is to show something representing something else that's really representing itself."

Allison coughed. "Again, what inverted means."

Sara looked at Allison, who winked. Then she looked at Ian. "Got it. It's an inverted metaphor."

Jane stood up. "Okay, maybe we should go work on this back at the hotel." She looked at Ian. "Thank you so much for the help."

"But of course. Should you require added assistance, merely ask."

After Stygian Teal left the greenroom Rick and Steve joined Rod, Allison, and Ian.

Rick carried a bottle of water and a small handbag. He looked at Ian. "Did you figure it out?"

Before Ian could answer, Rod interjected. "He didn't ask."

Ian grimaced. "Never had the chance, mate."

Steve sat on one of the folding chairs. "What do we know?"

"It could be Sara. She doesn't know who her dad is," Allison added.

"You're sure?" Ian asked.

"Yeah. I'm sure."

"Bloody hell. I thought it was Jane. She doesn't know her father." Ian shook his head. "And she's the lead singer, which has to be some kind of heritable trait."

"What about Kara and Indira?" Allison asked. "Maybe we should find out about them."

The men nodded, not certain who would be tasked with the interrogation. Before anyone could volunteer, Sy stepped in the room, clipboard in one hand, cell phone in the other. She pointed to the door. "Your ride is here."

The warehouse was remarkably nondescript, even for a warehouse. No identification of who owned it, what might be inside, or whether it was occupied was apparent on its concrete exterior.

Joji parked in his van in a large loading dock, found the only door on the building, and knocked. No one answered. He knocked again. After several minutes the door opened. A man wearing matching black Adidas sweatpants and sweatshirt stood in the door. He had a large scar on the side of his face and tattoos across his neck.

"Are you here to work?" the man with the scar asked.

"Yes. I'm Joji."

The man with the scar took Joji's arm and pulled him inside. "When you work here, you stay here, unless you are told to leave."

"Okay. No breaks?"

The man grimaced. "You can take breaks. You just can't leave until you are told to."

Joji nodded his head.

The man led Joji through a maze of boxes and crates to a small office in the middle of the warehouse. Inside three men sat at a small table smoking. One wore a tan suit and blue tie. The others were dressed in black Adidas sweatsuits just like the man who had let Joji into the warehouse.

The man in the tan suit pointed toward the back of the warehouse. "Put him to work there, with the others."

Joji followed one of the men in the sweatsuits to an area in the warehouse where a large pile of boxes had been unloaded from a truck. The boxes were all labeled "ramen" in blue and gold letters. Three men were putting the boxes onto carts and rolling them to a large series of shelves where they were being added to other boxes of ramen. The man pointed to the boxes, turned, and headed back to the office. Joji began to load the boxes of ramen with the other men.

After moving boxes of ramen, a truck delivered boxes of bonito flakes. Another followed with canned tomatoes. Then another with dried miso soup. And so on. By afternoon Joji figured he had picked up and moved nearly every kind of dried or canned food sold in Kobe.

Late in the day, the man in the tan suit emerged from the office and stood near a loading bay. Every half hour or so a truck would arrive. The driver would emerge from the truck, hand the man in the suit a wad of cash, and give a list to one of the men in the Adidas sweatsuits. The men in the sweatsuits would direct Joji and the other workers to fetch various items from the warehouse shelves and put them onto the arriving trucks.

At the end of the day the man in the suit gave each of the workers some money and sent them home. Joji thanked the men and returned to his van, where he promptly fell asleep. The next day and the day after that, he returned to the warehouse where he spent another day unloading trucks.

Very early on the third morning Joji was unloading a truck when he saw a man lying on the floor in the back of the truck behind some boxes. He was blindfolded and his hands and feet were tied with a white cord. Joji touched his leg to make sure he was alive. The man moved.

"Are you okay?" Joji asked.

"I'm fine, leave me alone," the man replied.

"Should I tell someone you are tied up?" Joji asked.

"No. They know I'm tied up."

Joji moved toward the man. "Well let me at least untie you."

"Please don't. I won't get paid unless I'm tied up."

"You get paid for being tied up?"

"Yes. They take the truck and empty it and return it with me tied up in the back. That's how it works."

Joji paused, uncertain what to do. It hadn't occurred to him that the trucks were full of stolen merchandise, or that he might be participating in an illegal activity. As he stood looking at the tied-up man trying to decide what to do, he felt the truck begin to violently shake.

———————

For about twenty minutes Joji wasn't certain what was happening. He fell to the floor of the truck. Several times he tried to stand but was knocked to the ground again and again. He could see boxes in the warehouse falling off shelves and the other workers on the ground covering their heads. The lights flickered on and off a few times before going dark. The tied-up man started screaming.

After the shaking stopped Joji carefully stood up. He reached over to the man and started to untie his hands and feet. The man didn't object and removed his blindfold.

Joji and the previously tied-up man made their way out of the truck and into the warehouse. Boxes that had been organized on shelves were scattered around the warehouse floor. One of the large shelving racks had been overturned and lay on its side. The other workers pulled themselves up and staggered toward the door. A man in a sweatsuit crawled out of the office and carefully stood up. He yelled something at the workers who were trying to leave and pulled a gun out of his jacket. The workers didn't stop. They ran through the door even as the man in the sweatsuit fired a round in their direction.

Joji walked toward the man in the sweatsuit and held up his hands. The man put his gun back in his jacket.

"Is everyone okay?" Joji asked, pointing toward the office.

The man in the sweatsuit didn't answer but turned and stepped back into the office. Inside the two other men in sweatsuits were still on the floor, one with a large gash on his forehead. The man in the tan suit was huddled underneath the desk.

Joji helped the men in sweatsuits off the floor and found some tissues. He held them over the wound on the man's head. He reached under the desk and coaxed the man in the tan suit out.

After they had brushed themselves off, the four men and Joji walked through the warehouse door. As they stepped outside each man looked with horror at their surroundings. For as far as the eye could see, every second or third building had turned to rubble. Electrical lines, once festooned overhead, lay on the street. Water bubbled up on the street from broken mains beneath. A truck in the middle of the street lay crushed by a large pole that had fallen. A few other people stood outside the buildings in which they had been working, viewing the destruction with shock and awe.

Joji's van, along with most of the vehicles in the warehouse lot, appeared untouched.

For the next several hours, Joji, the men in the Adidas sweatsuits, and the man in the tan suit wandered the streets of Kobe. Where buildings had fallen, people dug through the rubble trying to extricate those trapped inside. In some areas fires had started that, without the help of the local fire brigade, were unchecked and began to spread. Every hour or so an aftershock rattled the structure that had survived the initial quake. Everywhere people were crying or screaming for help.

———————

Joji, the man in the tan suit, and the men in the Adidas sweatsuits appeared numb when they returned to the warehouse. One sat on a curb staring off into space. The man in the tan suit had taken off his jacket and tie. He leaned against a post smoking a cigarette with a shaky hand. Hours passed. Night fell. In the distance the glow of fires lit up the night sky.

Early the next morning a man with dusty clothes and flushed face wandered down the street. He approached Joji and the men. "Can you help me find my son?" he asked.

The man in the tan suit looked at him contemptuously. "Your son is dead. Everyone is dead."

The man shook his head. "No, I can hear his cries. He is stuck underneath my house. He is alive but if I cannot get him, he will be dead."

Joji stood up. "I will help you. Where is your house?" He pointed to the men with the Adidas jumpsuits. "They will help you as well."

The man with the dusty clothes started to cry. "Thank you. Thank you. My son is all I have. Thank you."

The men in the Adidas sweatsuits looked at each other. One of them shrugged. They stood.

Joji retrieved his van. The man with the dusty clothes and the men in the sweatsuits climbed aboard.

When they arrived at the man's house a small crowd had gathered. A few neighbors were pulling buckets of rubble from the house and digging with their hands. Joji and the men from the warehouse began pulling pieces of wood and plaster away from the site.

Every few minutes one of the neighbors would lay flat on the rubble and everyone stopped digging. After a moment they would raise their hand and the work would continue once again.

After an hour or so, one of the men in the Adidas sweatsuits approached Joji. "We need shovels and tools. There are some at the warehouse. Go get them and bring them here." Joji nodded and turned to his van. When he returned with shovels and other digging tools the crowd had become frantic. "No one has heard a sound for the last half hour," someone replied when Joji asked.

Several minutes later one of the men in an Adidas sweatsuit shouted, "I see his arm!" Everyone stopped. The man who saw the arm dropped to his knees and began digging with his hands. The others crowded around, being careful not to dislodge any rubble that might further bury the child.

The crowd gasped a few moments later when the man pulled a small child, no more than five or six years old, out of the crushed stone and wood. The child was covered from head to toe in dust and was nearly limp. Someone poured some water on the child's face and he opened his eyes and began to sit up. Those who had been digging applauded as the man in the sweatsuit handed the boy to his father.

As Joji watched, the crowd gathered round the men in the Adidas sweatsuits. Many of the people in the crowd bowed. Several quietly mumbled "yuusha" (hero). The men in the sweatsuits looked surprised, unsure how to respond. They shook hands with the boy's father and made their way back toward Joji. As they did, a small elderly woman wearing a frock stood in front of them and bowed deeply.

"People in this part of the city are very poor. When help comes it will not come for us. Thank you for what you have done."

The men looked uncomfortable. One of them bowed. The woman smiled and turned back toward the crowd.

The ride back to the warehouse was quiet. When they arrived, Joji found a bottle of water and some dried fish flakes. He ate them next to his van, and as the sun began to drop in the sky he fell into a deep sleep.

The next morning, he was awakened by the man in the tan suit, now in shirt sleeves. The men in Adidas sweatsuits stood next to him, each holding a large box.

"Get up," the man in shirt sleeves demanded.

Joji sat straight up

Without a word the men in the sweatsuits put the boxes in the back of the van and climbed in. "Drive," one of them ordered.

Joji turned on his van and began to pull out of the warehouse parking lot.

"Where am I going?" Joji asked.

"Where were we yesterday?" one of the men replied.

When Joji's van arrived back where the boy was pulled from the rubble, neighbors were still digging through the remnants of their homes, looking for whatever they could find. Possessions, mementos, food, or any bit of life that might have provided a sliver of hope that their current predicament would improve were sought with a silent fervor.

They pointed Joji toward a four-way stop and told him to park his van. When he did, the men got out, unloaded the boxes, and opened them. None of the people in the area paid attention as they did. The men in the sweatsuits weren't sure what to do. "Hey," one shouted. "We have food."

A few heads turned and a pair of elderly women shuffled toward the van. The men picked up a can and a couple packets of ramen and handed them to each of the women. Slowly others began to appear, silently making their way to the van. Within a half hour a line formed, and the men were quickly running out of food to hand out. One of them pointed to Joji. "Bring back more."

Joji left and returned to the warehouse. He found several more boxes of various foods. He put them in the van and drove back to the men. By the time he arrived a small crowd had gathered. The men in the Adidas sweatsuits were pushing people into a line, pointing menacingly whenever someone stepped out of place.

Joji pulled up the van and began unloading the boxes.

One of the men sternly asked, "How many more boxes are in the warehouse?"

Joji wasn't sure how to answer. After all, the warehouse was filled with boxes of food. "There are a lot of boxes left," he replied. "We could bring some more."

"Not here," the man answered. "There are other people in the city."

The next day a man in gray trousers came to the warehouse with a small truck. Joji and the men in the sweatsuits (which they hadn't changed since the earthquake) set off to a different neighborhood. They handed out food to a surprised crowd. The next day a different neighborhood and later that day another.

On the fourth day the man in the tan suit called Joji and the men in the Adidas sweatsuits. "It's time we organized better. We don't have enough trucks to visit all the people. It's time we figure out how to bring them here." He turned to Joji. "You are now part of Sumiyoshi-kai."

"Thank you," Joji replied.

One of the men in a sweatsuit added, "You'll need to get a tattoo of the diamond." He pulled up his sleeve to reveal a kanji surrounded by a sun.

Joji nodded, uncertain if he was really going to have to get a tattoo. "I'll get my van and spread the word."

The man in the tan suit nodded.

"I have a question," Joji said. "I don't know your names. If I'm joining the organization, I probably should know your names."

The man in the tan suit looked directly at Joji. "We don't have names."

Joji's eyes grew wide. "I understand. You, we, are the Sumiyoshi-kai. No names."

———————

For the next month the warehouse became a focal point for the citizens of Kobe. Every morning a line of people waited in the parking lot until the warehouse door opened and men wearing Adidas sweatsuits distributed food. When the International Red Cross asked a representative in the Japanese government what kind of charity Sumiyoshi was and whether there were individuals who might be interested in helping the Red Cross, a government official politely responded he would find out. He never replied.

CHAPTER 7

Takeshi's Castle

Into the fishbowl dungeon I fall
On the stage I see myself
Alone above the crowd I see, my soul in thrall

—Uncle Joe's Band, "On the Tele"

The morning after the first show, the two bands and Sy met for breakfast in a small room at one end of the hotel. The breakfast was remarkably un-Japanese, save for the generous helpings of rice. After a few pleasantries Sy stood and pulled out a piece of paper. "Okay, Stygian Teal, you'll be heading north. Today you'll be off. I've got some time set up for you at an onsen."

Jane looked up. "An onsen?"

"It's like a spa. You'll enjoy it."

Sy looked down at her notes. "And Uncle Joe's Band will be doing a promotional visit."

Rod coughed. "What exactly have you gotten us into this time?"

Sy smiled. "What do you mean?"

The four members of Uncle Joe's Band stopped eating all at once and stared at Sy.

"Like when you had us compete in the haggis eating contest in Edinburgh?" Rod replied.

"Or officiating a pro wrestling match in Guadalajara?" Steve added.

"How about crocodile wrangling in Australia?" Rick looked at a scar on his arm.

Rod nodded in agreement. "Don't forget the elephant ride in Bangkok."

Ian tilted his head. "I didn't think the elephant ride was that bad."

Rod leaned across the table. "It's inhumane. For the elephant."

Sy smiled. "Don't worry. This one will be easy. You're going to be on a game show."

Uncle Joe's Band said nothing.

"It's one of the oldest and most famous shows in Japan, *Takeshi's Castle.*"

Rod sat back in his chair. "That doesn't sound bad. We go on television, answer some questions, have a quick laugh, make like we know what's going on, and talk about our album."

"Exactly," Sy responded. "Not bad at all."

———————

Uncle Joe's Band arrived at the studio where *Takeshi's Castle* was filmed and was greeted by a short man in a brown suit. He bowed. "My name is Gary. I'll be your guide and translator today." He shook each band member's hand. "Let me show you to the preparation room."

Rod nudged Steve. "Did he say, 'preparation room'?"

"I think so."

Gary led the band down a short corridor to a room filled with props. A large spider hung from the ceiling. Paper mache cakes sat on shelves along with a clown face, a giant pen, a confetti gun, and dozens of other items.

Ian looked up on the wall near the room. "Not exactly what I'd expected for a bloody game show. Thought we might see a few trivia questions, maybe a bunch of computer monitors or something."

Rod tapped Gary's arm. "Gary. How do you play Takeshi's castle?"

Gary turned, stopped walking, and looked at the band. "Rod-san, it is very simple. You must storm Baron Takeshi's castle. If you manage to get to the castle you win."

A man in a red shirt handed white jumpsuits to the band-mates. He held each jumpsuit up to ensure it would fit before bowing and handing it to the band member.

As the band put on their jumpsuits Rod tapped Gary's arm again. "Gary, how do we get to Takeshi's castle?"

Gary smiled. "Rod-san, you simply follow the general. He will tell you how to get there."

"Do we answer questions?" Rod asked.

"Sometimes. Every game is different."

The man who gave the band white jumpsuits returned, this time with red helmets.

Ian looked at Rick. "Why do we need helmets?"

Rick grimaced. "I don't like this."

———————

Adorned in their helmets and jumpsuits the band was escorted into a forested area behind the studio. Dozens of other people milled around a large meadow. All wore the same white jumpsuits and red helmets.

"What do we do now?" Ian asked nervously.

"We wait for the general," replied Gary.

As he finished answering Ian, a man in a military uniform stepped up on a large rock in the middle of the field. Gary jumped to attention. "It's General Tani!" The crowd cheered.

General Tani began to speak to the crowd. Gary translated. "You are all being pressed into service. I am General Tani and you will be my army!" He pointed toward the band, "We have special guests here today. The American rock and roll band, Uncle Joe! Maybe they will sing their way to the castle first!" The crowd politely clapped. "We will assault the castle today. Takeshi has created many barriers around his castle. Are you ready!" The general raised his fist. "Go!" He pointed toward a road leading away from the meadow. En masse the white jumpsuited, red helmeted game show contestants began running down the road.

"What do we do?" Rod asked.

Gary, raising his arms in excitement, yelled, "Go, Rod-san, Go!"

Ian looked at Steve. "Fine. But I'm bloody hell not running."

The four men followed the crowd. A short distance down the road the crowd was gathered around a steep barrier covered in black plastic. At the base of the plastic was a large pit filled with muddy water. The crowd of contestants had entered the water and was diligently trying to climb up the plastic-covered barrier. The barrier was slippery and as individuals tried to scale the barrier, they would slide back down into the muddy water pit.

Rick looked at the spectacle. "I'm not doing that. I don't care what Sy said we were going to do. I'm not doing that."

Steve looked at the crowd. Several cameramen stood close to the action filming every crash, slide, and fall into the watery pit. He tapped Ian's shoulder and pointed toward a path that led along one side of the barrier. Well versed from years of working in rowdy clubs requiring clandestine escapes after shows, Uncle Joe's Band slipped past the cameramen and the crowd and made their way to the other side of the barrier.

A few hundred feet past the first obstacle stood a white building surrounded on two sides by trenches filled with water. Gary stood near the door at the front of the building. He clapped his hands in excitement as the band approached.

"You made it over the slippery hill," he said. "Only eight-five percent of contestants get past the first obstacle." He pointed at a door on the white building. "Next is the labyrinth. It is filled with small rooms. Each room has six doors. You must make your way through the maze and escape to the other side. If you go the wrong way you will fall into the water pit."

"That's it?" Rick asked.

Gary held up a finger with a mischievous grin. "And there are monsters. Don't let the monsters find you."

Ian sighed, "Uh, mate, we don't *do* monsters."

Gary giggled. "This is good, Ian-san. Monsters are bad. Don't let them find you."

Rick shook his head and opened the door. "Let's get this over with," he muttered.

The "maze" was a series of cheaply built rooms with plywood doors connecting one room to the next. Each room was hexagonal, with six doors creating the appearance from above of a giant honeycomb. There was no roof on the building, allowing a series of cameras hoisted on booms to look down on the contestants as they made their way through the labyrinth.

The band members casually walked from room to room, making their way toward the far end of the building. As Steve stepped from one room to the next a large man in red tights with an orange wig holding a paper mache club jumped out from the shadows. He roared menacingly.

Seedy bars and other decrepit establishments had left Uncle Joe's Band with a sense of self-preservation and quick reactions to personal safety not well known by many game show contestants. Thus, it wasn't a surprise that when the "monster" roared at Rick, his initial response wasn't to run, or to cry out, but to throw a left uppercut to the man's jaw. The actor dressed in red tights fell backwards into the room from which he had just emerged.

"What was that?" Rod asked as he stepped in the room behind Rick.

"Nothing," Rick replied. "Stupid game show annoyance."

As the band moved further through the maze another "monster" emerged. Instead of red tights, a leopard skin tunic crossed the chest of another large man wearing a minotaur-shaped helmet. Equally unfazed and reactionary as Rick, Steve and Ian quickly had the man gasping for breath, holding his ribs. The camera crew monitoring the water pit outside the building was surprised when, rather than a contestant being thrown into the water pit by a large actor dressed as a monster, it was the actor landing face-first in the muddy water.

As Uncle Joe's Band emerged from the maze, Gary's eyes grew in amazement. "Only fifteen percent of contestants make it through the maze," he said. "You have made it to the walls of Takeshi's castle."

The bandmates made their way to Takeshi's castle in an increasingly foul mood. The "castle" was little more than a facade of a castle sitting on a small island in the middle of a pond. In the castle "moat" were several blow-up kayaks, each large enough for two people.

Gary pointed to the kayaks. "All you have to do now is take those boats and row across the moat."

Steve grimaced. "What about the other boats?"

"They will have Takeshi's men trying to stop you." As he spoke several individuals wearing demon-like masks dressed in black robes appeared from the castle and began to get into the blow-up kayaks on the castle side of the moat. Another group of mask-wearing individuals stood on the shore, each with a bucket next to them.

Rod cleared his throat. "Gary."

"Yes, Rod-san."

"How are they going to try and stop us?"

"They will throw things at you; they will try and tip over your boats," Gary said with an enthusiastic look on his face.

Ian pulled one of the kayaks up on the shore. "Gents, I say we bloody well get this over with. What say you?"

Steve nodded. "Damn right. Let's get to the other side and get this done."

Rod and Steve climbed into one boat while Rick and Ian sat in the other. For a moment, the actors in their demon-masks and Uncle Joe's Band stared across the water at each other. Then with a series of loud yells the demon-mask-wearing actors began to row their kayaks toward the band.

It was clear that the actors in their demonic costumes had generally pursued the other contestants, who, hoping to win, did everything possible to row away. In contrast, the band, instead of rowing away, pushed forward, directly toward Takeshi's demon guard. On the shore the demon guards began to throw small plastic balls at the band. When the boat got closer Ian felt the edge of his oar. It was sharper than he expected.

As one of the demon boats got close to Ian's he stopped rowing, took his oar, and hit the side of their boat. A loud "*pop*" ensued. The demons who had tried to look menacing now twisted their heads around, wondering what had just happened. As the air let out of the blow-up kayak the demons found themselves neck deep in water. Steve, who was watching the sinking of the kayak, took his oar and hit another boat. It, too, exploded and sank. The remaining demons looked at their comrades neck deep in water and began rowing in the other direction. As they did, those on shore continued to throw more and more of the plastic balls at the band's boat. One flew close enough to Rick that he reached out and caught it. He looked at it in his hand and then threw it back at those on the shore. It hit the actor's mask and he staggered backward.

Rod caught a ball and did the same. Soon balls were flying back and forth. The actors trying to unseat the band were pummeled by their own projectiles. They began to slowly back away from the shore.

When their boats hit the shore, Ian leapt from his boat paddle in hand, and chased the actors toward the castle. One of the actors tripped on his cloak and fell against Takeshi's castle. With a loud crack the facade began to twist and fall. A crash ensued as Takeshi's castle fell to the ground.

Joji drove for hours to get to Hakuba, in the north of the Japanese archipelago. The small town was becoming inundated with visitors preparing for the 1998 Winter Olympics in nearby Nagano. The town's few hotels were filled and visitors milled about the town waiting for the games to start in earnest.

It was simple curiosity that led Joji to the games. Never having had any athletic prowess or interest in sport, he was always delighted by spectacle. And if the Olympic games were known for anything, it was a spectacle.

When he arrived in Hakuba, Joji found a small garage next to an old noodle factory. He parked his van, climbed into the back, and promptly went to sleep. The next morning, he arose to find a fresh blanket of snow covering the ground. It crunched as he walked down the street to a ramen house. As he sat down with a large, steaming bowl of noodles bathed in an onion and shrimp broth a man stepped into the small restaurant. He looked distinctly out of place, not simply because of his colorful red, green, and black jacket, or red and green scarf. He looked for a place to sit and when unable to find one pointed to the seat at the table across from Joji.

Joji nodded and stood to make space. The man was clearly a foreigner, and as most non-Japanese couldn't speak Japanese, Joji introduced himself in the only other language he knew, English. "Hello, my name is Joji."

Much to Joji's delight the man responded in English. "Hello, Joji, my name is Phillip. Thank you for allowing me to sit with you."

Joji nodded and waved at the waiter, who handed a menu to Phillip.

Joji couldn't remember the English word for pork. "You should try the shrimp or pig. They are very good."

Phillip's face broke into a wide infectious smile. "Thank you. I will try the pig." He pointed to a picture on the menu. The waiter nodded, took the menu, and walked back to the kitchen.

"Where are you from?" Joji asked.

"Kenya," Phillip replied, pointing at a small Kenyan flag on his jacket. "I'm here for the Olympics.

"Oh. Very exciting." Joji nodded. "Are you competing?"

"Yes. I will compete tomorrow," Philip responded.

"What competing do you do?"

"Cross-country skiing. I am skiing in the ten-kilometer race."

The waiter set a steaming bowl of ramen in front of Philip.

"Do you ski in Kenya?"

Phillip slurped some of the ramen. "No. There is no skiing in Kenya."

Joji tilted his head. "How did you learn to ski? And how are you competing in cross-country skiing?"

Philip coughed a little. "I was a middle-distance runner. A good one. I won many races. One day a man came to me from a shoe company, Nike." Philip pointed at his Nike shoes. "He said the company wanted me to learn to try skiing and that they would pay for me to learn. I agreed. Nike sent me to Finland where I learned to ski." He took a large gulp of broth. "And now I am here."

Joji sat up, intrigued. "Did you come here with a team?"

Philip shook his head. "No. No team. There is no team from Kenya. There isn't even a team from Africa. I will be the first."

Joji's eyes widened. "The first skier from Kenya?"

"No. The first African in the Winter Olympics."

Joji looked at Philip, who in their short conversation had managed to nearly finish his ramen. "Are you excited for the race tomorrow?"

Philip suddenly had a worried look on his face. "I am excited but I'm not sure how I'm going to get there. The other teams all have vans for their skis and people to help them. I am alone."

Joji smiled. "I have a van. I will join your team."

Philip stood up and took Joji's hand. "That would be amazing. I cannot thank you enough. Welcome to Team Kenya."

———

If Philip was disappointed when he saw Joji's van, he didn't show it. Joji met him at his hotel early the next morning. After putting his equipment in the van, Team Kenya made its way to the Olympic cross-country ski course. The course was next to an onsen known as Snow Harp in Nozawa. The road to the course was slippery owing less to snow and ice and more to the rain that had begun to fall.

Philip was excited but appeared a bit worried. "The rain will make the snow sticky, like mud. It clings to the skis."

When Joji's van pulled up to the team entrance, a guard holding a clipboard looked skeptically at the van and asked for identification. Philip held up a card, which the guard looked at carefully. "What team are you?" he asked Joji in Japanese.

"We are Team Kenya," Joji said with a smile.

The guard glared at the van. Without a word he waved them into the team parking lot.

Joji helped Philip prepare his skis and put on his racing bib. As the athletes prepared to start, Joji led Philip to the track. The other teams looked with curiosity as an African skier and his helper, a small Japanese man not wearing a winter coat or hat, made their way to the starting line.

As each racer was introduced the crowd clapped politely. Philip was introduced last.

The ten-kilometer cross-country race at the 1998 Nagano Winter Olympics is often cited as the greatest example of the Olympic spirit in the modern era.

As the race began it was apparent the snow was not ideal. More of a thick slush than icy surface, it slowed the entire field. Champion cross-country skier Bjorn Daehlie, who had won the ten-kilometer race in the prior Olympiad, jumped into the lead early, where he remained. The victory was his sixth, the most of any Winter Olympian. As fans and broadcasters reveled in the historic victory, officials started the medal ceremony before the race had fully concluded, eager to ensure it occurred in time for the television networks to carry the event. But as they prepared to present the gold medal, Bjorn was nowhere near the medal podium.

The final racer in the field, Philip Boit, the first African to participate in the Winter Olympics, made it to the finish line in forty-seven minutes and twenty-five seconds, twenty minutes after Bjorn. As he crossed the finish line Bjorn met Philip, gave him a high-five, and patted him on the back. For a moment the entirety of the competitors, the crowd, even the television audience forgot about the medal ceremony and remembered exactly why the Olympics existed in the first place. Over the ensuing years Philip and Bjorn became close friends. Philip competed in subsequent winter games in Salt Lake

City and Turin, never winning, but managing to avoid last place. He retired from cross-country skiing in 2010.

As he left the parking lot late that night, Joji stopped near the entrance. On the side of a building near the grandstand he painted in white:

Glorious winter
On snow, bold skis flying
Out of Africa

———————

When Uncle Joe's Band arrived at their hotel in Kobe, Sy met them in the lobby.

"How was the game show?"

Rod handed her a muddy towel. "We won."

Sy set the towel on a table. "That's great. We'll use it as a promotional angle."

Ian coughed. "I wouldn't do that, mate."

"A few video clips of you answering some trivia questions will go over well. I'm sure we can find some that will work."

Steve flopped down on one of the large chairs in the center of the lobby. "Sy, have you ever seen *Takeshi's Castle*?"

"No. Why?"

Rick folded his arms. "There weren't any trivia questions. It was more like a giant obstacle course."

Sy smiled. "Even better. Seeing you guys run through some big obstacles will make the news."

Ian crossed his arms. "How should I put this? After we won the bloody thing, they told us we were probably going to be sued and that we might have committed a felony."

"And that we were never allowed back. Ever. Under any circumstances. Ever," Rod added.

Sy's smile twisted and she raised one of her eyebrows. "Let me see, the hard metal rock band members go on a game show, misbehave, destroy things, and get themselves banned from ever returning."

The band nodded in agreement.

Sy's eyes twinkled. "As would be expected from a rebellious, loud, culturally challenged group."

The band members were silent.

"Sounds like a perfect outing to me," Sy uttered as she walked away.

CHAPTER 8

The Andon Cord

Autumn factory
For a human, great heart build
Watching the spark plug

—Jo Ojisan

As Uncle Joe's Band was making its way to *Takeshi's Castle*, Stygian Teal drove to the Sunrise Onsen. Allison, as a reward for her translation and introduction skills, joined the four band members. The van arrived at the onsen in the middle of the morning.

"This place is like a spa?" Jane asked as they entered an older building with a decrepit yellow facade.

Allison opened a large wooden door in the front of the building. "I think so. I've read about these places. Everyone says they are a cross between a spa and a public bathhouse."

"I'm not sure if I'm encouraged or not," Kara replied.

Inside the entrance to the spa a woman in a kimono met the band, bowed, and motioned for the band members to follow her. She led them to a small room with towels, robes, and slippers.

"What do we do?" Kara asked.

"I'm pretty sure we put these on," Allison said as she picked up a robe.

Jane crossed her arms. "I'm not changing into these."

"It's a freaking spa. You put on the robe and the slippers and get a massage or treatment or get wrapped in seaweed," Sara said, pulling off her shirt.

"Ugh. Fine." Jane picked up a robe and slippers.

When the band members and Allison had finished changing

into robes and slippers, they walked down a short hallway to a large room with a series of small stations and a large pool of water. Each station had a stool sitting in front of a faucet, a spigot, and a small shelf lined with various soaps, shampoos, and cleansers. A bucket and scrub brush sat next to each stool.

"This looks like a place you would wash your dog," Indira quipped.

A few women were sitting at the stations, washing their hair, using the brush to scrub their backs, soaping and cleansing. Occasionally one of the women would take a bucket, fill it with water, and dump it over her head.

The pool varied in depth from a few feet on one end to neck deep on the other. Women lounged in small groups, chatting in low voices.

"What do we do?" Sara asked.

Allison cleared her throat. "Just do what everyone else is doing. Wash first and then get in the pool."

With that, each of the band members found a stool and began to wash.

———————

Late one afternoon in mid-October 1977, Jo Ojisan's van began to shake. For many years the van had run with little difficulty, despite the minimal amount of servicing and maintenance it had undergone.

Joji wasn't entirely certain what to do when the van's symptoms seemed to worsen. His knowledge of automotive repair was modest and he decided the best approach was to actively seek help from the most knowledgeable experts he could find.

As he drove toward Kobe, Joji noticed a Toyota sign over a large building. He pulled off the road toward the building, where he was stopped at a gate by a serious-looking security guard.

"Where are you going?" the guard asked in a gruff voice.

"To find a van expert."

The guard looked at the van. "This is a factory, not a repair shop."

Joji thought for a moment. "Does the .factory have van experts?"

"Yes. They have the best experts."

Joji smiled. "Perfect."

The guard waited a moment, unsure how to respond. Finally, he pointed at Joji. "They don't have time to see you."

Joji thought for a moment. "Did you ask them?"

The guard gave a loud "humph," turned, and walked back toward the factory. After a few minutes he returned, opened the gate, and stood by as Joji drove in.

Joji wasn't sure where to find the van expert who would stop his van from shaking, so he drove around the factory until he found a large parking lot filled with new Toyota vans. Sitting in his van for a half hour, he noted how a new van left the factory through a large door every five minutes or so.

After one of the new vans exited the doors, Joji drove his decidedly older van through the doors and into the factory. He stopped and parked his van in front of a small group of workers. They stopped what they were doing and walked around Joji's van, unsure why it had entered their factory.

Joji stepped out of his van and looked at the group of workers. They all wore matching jumpsuits, hardhats, and goggles. One held a wrench, another a clipboard.

"Which one of you is a van expert?" Joji asked.

The workers looked at each other without responding.

"Do you know where I can find someone who is an expert at fixing vans?" Joji asked again.

One of the workers pointed down a long assembly line toward a small office near the far end of the building. Joji shrugged and started walking. As he made his way across the giant concrete floor he watched as men pulled parts off one machine and put them on the next, cut, and welded metal, and attached one part to another.

As Joji walked he noticed along the walkway next to the assembly line was a red cord. The cord was suspended a few feet above the workers heads and ran the entire length of the factory. At nearly every workstation it dipped low enough it could be easily reached.

When he reached the office, Joji knocked on the door. A man in white shirt sleeves and black tie wearing a hardhat opened it. "Can I help you?"

"I'm looking for someone who can fix a Subaru van."

The man in the shirt sleeves looked past Joji. "Everyone here can fix a Toyota van. But not Subaru vans. We build Toyotas."

Joji grimaced. "Aren't Toyotas and Subarus basically the same?"

"No. No, they are not."

Joji smiled. "Well, perhaps you could just look at it. My van is down there." He pointed to the far end of the factory. "Maybe you could tell me how to fix it."

The man in the shirt sleeves frowned. "I am too busy to fix your van. Find someone else." He closed the door.

Joji turned and looked at the assembly line. In every workspace were the "experts" he assumed could fix his van. He stopped at a station where three men were assembling part of a drive shaft. They didn't notice until he tapped one on the shoulder.

The man looked up, startled. "What?"

Joji smiled. "You are a van expert. Can you come help fix my van?"

The man grimaced. "We are busy. I don't have time to stop and look at your van." He pointed to the assembly line. "Can't you see? The line never stops. Neither do we." The man turned around and continued to work on the drive shaft.

Joji turned and began walking back down the walkway. After he passed several more workstations a thought occurred to him. He tapped another worker on the shoulder. "How do you get the line to stop?" he asked.

Much to Joji's surprise the worker pointed at the red cord above his head. "Andon," he replied and turned back toward his workstation.

Joji thought for a moment. Finally, with a shrug he reached up and grabbed the cord and pulled it. As he did, he heard a loud, blaring horn and looked to see a flashing red light go off somewhere above his head. He let go of the cord and stepped back. As if on cue, the entire assembly line stopped. Workers in every station stepped away from whatever they had been building.

In the distance he could see men in white shirts sleeves and hardhats holding clipboards emerge en masse from the office. They began to fan out across the factory floor, stopping at each workstation quickly, asking pointed questions to the workers. Joji continued to march down the walkway, watching in amazement as the workers stood waiting for the men with clipboards. After several minutes the flashing red light turned blue, and the horn stopped blaring. The workers all started working again.

Joji made his way back to his van. Near the end of the line, he stopped at a workstation. He raised his hand and a worker looked up. "Hi. Can you help me fix my van?"

The worker shook his head. "Too busy," he replied.

Joji smiled. "No problem." He reached up and pulled the Andon cord. The red light and blazing horn echoed across the factory as work stopped once again. The men with clipboards rushed from the office, this time looking frustrated.

The worker who had told Joji he was too busy gasped and shook his head. "You should not have done that."

"Why not? Now you can come and look at my van." Joji replied.

The worker shook his head. "I can't leave my station."

Joji thought for a moment. "Do you need more time?" he asked. When the worker didn't respond Joji reached up and pulled on the cord again.

The worker tapped one of the men next to him on the arm and pointed at Joji. The two talked in low voices for a moment before turning back toward Joji. "Okay. Just don't pull the red cord again."

Joji smiled. "Okay."

The men set down their tools and followed Joji to his van. Joji turned it on and drove it around in a small circle while the three workers watched. The van began to shake. One of the workers motioned for Joji to stop driving. When he did, they opened the hood.

As they pulled the hood open the blue light began to flash and the assembly line started to grind on again. The men stopped and started back toward their workstation.

"Wait." Joji tried to wave at them as they began to walk away. He ran to the end of the Andon cord and pulled it again. Once again, the red light began to flash and the line stopped. The workers looked at each other. They turned back toward Joji's van.

"Please, please do not do that again," one of them pleaded.

"Oh, no problem. I just thought you needed more time," Joji replied. He pointed to his van. "Can you fix it?"

"If you stop pulling the Andon cord."

Joji nodded. "Of course."

The men began to look at Joji's van. With remarkable speed they removed pieces of the engine, removed the tires, and checked the brake pads. A few minutes after they started one of the workers raised a spark plug. He ran to a workstation and returned with a new plug. After the old spark plug had been replaced with the new, the workers put the van back together, turned over the engine and drove it around in a small circle. The shaking was gone.

Joji bowed as the men stepped out of the van and returned to their workstations. After he drove through the front gates of the factory he stopped. With his brush and white paint, he wrote in large kanji's:

Autumn factory
For a human, great heart build
Watching the spark plug

Over the ensuing two years workers walked past the poem, gradually accepting it as a mantra. Managers recited it at company events. Visitors to the factory would have their pictures taken next to it. Toyota's chairman had a giant black and white photograph of Joji's haiku hung in the company's headquarters. In time the words became a symbol of the Japanese factory workers' dedication and spirit. The legend of Jo Ojisan grew.

"Did you always want to be in a band?" Allison asked as she and Indira sat in the deep end of the onsen pool.

"No. I started playing an upright bass in my high school orchestra. It was too heavy to carry to school, so I switched to the bass guitar."

"How hard was it to change?"

"Not hard. They're basically the same instrument. Just one is a lot smaller and you play it on its side."

Allison nodded. "Did you like the orchestra?"

"It was okay. My mom wanted me to play the violin, but I never wanted to. It was one of those things you just do because you're told it's a good idea. Good for your future and all that."

"Did your dad like the orchestra?"

Indira smiled. "Yes, he did. My stepdad, actually. My stepdad was really into it. He'd take me to orchestra concerts all the time. We'd get seats really close to the stage so we could fully absorb the sound."

Allison pulled herself up on the pool deck. "I never got to do stuff with my dad until a few years ago. Didn't know him."

"That's kind of strange."

"Yeah, I live with my grandparents and my mom isn't around much. I didn't know my dad, Rod, until a few years ago when my mom sent me to live with him for the summer."

"You lived with Uncle Joe's Band? That must have been so cool."

Allison smirked. "It was a little rough at first. They were a bit overbearing. And the places they played were pretty scary."

Indira smiled. "We've probably played in many of the same places."

"My dad smashed a guitar over a guy's head one time. Said he didn't like the look of him."

"Wow. That must have been a great show."

"Yeah, the police came and everything. No one was arrested, but the guy was knocked out."

Indira laughed. "I can't imagine him using a perfectly good guitar as a club."

"He was a bit overprotective."

Indira sighed. "Wouldn't it be great if you could make the world stop for a moment and see what exactly it was that happened? Why did your dad decide to whack a guy with a guitar? Push a button maybe or pull a cord and everything comes to a stop."

Allison nodded. "Definitely."

CHAPTER 9

Phil Ojisan

Blue sodden winter
A high, sullen shoes making
on the factory

—Jo Ojisan

Despite Joji's meager lifestyle, he still required some form of financial backing. After all, gas is expensive in Japan and even the basic necessities cannot be obtained without recompense. And though his parents could have provided the means, they did not. The mercurial source of Joji's support came early in his travels, built on the formulation of a relationship with a benefactor that lasted for most of Joji's life.

When Joji left home in his late teens and began his gypsy journey up and down the Japanese archipelago, he tried numerous times to become formally employed, both as a means of sustaining himself and in an effort to incur acceptance within his family. For the briefest of periods, he followed a myriad of career paths: zookeeper, high-rise window washer, chemical engineer, race car mechanic, fish farmer, snowboard manufacturer, and so on. Each effort started with some minicom of interest, followed by a period of invested learning, ending with boredom and a desire to do anything other than the job at hand.

It was in the course of these vocational endeavors that Joji found himself at a shoe manufacturing plant on the outskirts of Kobe. Joji found the job when he nearly ran his van off the road trying to avoid an oncoming truck. He saw the name of the company on the side of the truck as it whizzed past and made his way to the company headquarters where he intended to lodge a complaint.

As he sat in what he thought was the complaint department

waiting for someone with whom he could discuss the rabid truck driver, a smiling young woman stuck a questionnaire in his hand and told him to fill it out. He did, assuming it was part of the company's complaint process. After sitting alone waiting for someone to talk to about the truck driver, he was called into a small office. A man behind a desk started asking him questions; where he was from, what kind of work experience he had and so on. Just as he was about to raise his fist and report the aggressive driving, the man behind the desk congratulated him and told him he should report to work at the factory the next day. Joji paused for a moment, surprised, as the man told him what his salary would be. Before he had time to respond, Joji found himself signing some papers and being escorted out of the man's office.

The bands met in Kobe for their second concert. As they sat in the hotel lobby Jane handed Ian a piece of paper.

"Well, what have we here?" Ian said, trying not to reveal any sign of the excitement he felt being presented with something from the lead singer (who might potentially be his daughter) of another band.

"We started working on a new song. I wanted your opinion on the lyrics." Jane pointed to the paper.

Ian pushed his sunglasses up his nose and carefully read the lines on the paper. He squinted and read them again. He read it a third time and mouthed the words. He leaned back in his chair. "These are, well, lyrical. Lyrical lyrics."

Jane nodded excitedly. "Yes. They're lyrics."

Ian set the paper down in front of him. "What exactly is the goal of these? These lyrics."

"They're a song."

"Yes, but what is their *purpose*?"

"To enthrall the audience. To elicit a heightened sense of self and enlightenment among the people who listen to the song." Jane paused. "And to sell lots of albums."

Ian sat back and looked as professorial as a long-haired, aged, spent-too-many-nights-up-late-in-clubs, musician could look. He crossed his legs and put the tips of his fingers together as though he were about to make a deep and insightful point. "The purpose of lyrics is to create an *idea*, morphologically speaking."

Jane tried not to look confused. "What does that mean?"

"It means you take an idea someone else had and you *morph* it into your idea." Ian leaned forward. "Think of it like it's just an idea and you're going to make it better."

Jane frowned. "That sounds like plagiarism."

Ian sighed. "Jane, you must understand. There are no *new* ideas. There are only refurbished old ones." He paused for a moment before continuing. "Our first hit was called 'Broken Slipper.' You heard it, I assume."

Jane nodded.

"The idea of Cinderella wasn't really ours; it's a fairy tale after all. We just took the idea and refurbished it a bit. The princess did not require the requisite prince. She was fighting against the patriarchy, her evil stepmother, and the religious zealotry of her fairy godmother. All great stuff. No new ideas, just improved old ones."

Jane sat back and looked at what she had written. "What I need to do is find a source idea. Something I can riff off. That's what you're saying?"

"Precisely."

At the factory Joji learned the company was a giant conglomerate and that he would be working in a factory that manufactured shoes. His first assignment was to run a machine that cut thin leather into the pieces that would eventually become the shoe body. Instructions on how to vary the sizes and colors of the leather pieces were provided, but Joji soon forgot them and began producing bits of leather that went well together and would prove to be the most attractive. Despite the monotony of the work Joji found himself engaged and for a brief period enjoyed his new job.

Joji learned from other workers that the shoes being manufactured were athletic shoes that were to be worn by athletes during athletic events to enhance their athleticism. Joji never participated in sports, nor found them particularly interesting, but liked the idea that the work he was doing would lead to the production of an item that could be used by people for an enjoyable purpose. He imagined the shoes being worn by people playing soccer and tennis.

The shoes produced at Joji's factory were sold under a variety of different brands. During the short period of Joji's employment, the brand Tiger was in production and was to be sold primarily in North America and Europe.

Occasionally different product representatives would come to the factory to assess the production, consider different colors and styles, and decide what might be particularly salable within their individual marketplace. As most employees and managers at the plant were only fluent in Japanese, Joji was often called upon either to translate or to take the guests on a tour of the factory.

One morning Joji was called into the manager's office and introduced to a tall, lean American from the west coast of the United States. He had a pale complexion and wore an ill-fitting suit that rested like a tarp over his lanky frame. The manager bowed as Joji entered the room. Joji bowed in response. The manager introduced the man as "Phillip" and told Joji to take him on a tour of the factory.

Joji bowed toward the man and shook his hand. "I'm Joji. It's nice to meet you," he said.

"Joji, I'm Phil Knight. But just call me Phil." Phil bowed.

Joji opened the door and escorted Phil toward the factory floor. "Is there anything specific you'd like to see, Phil-san?"

"I'd like to see how you manufacture the soles," Phil responded.

Joji made his way to one corner of the factory as Phil followed. "The soles are made from a kind of soft rubber. It's poured into forms and pressed into the shape of the sole," Joji said as he pointed at a group of large machines with steam being emitted from them.

Phil walked around one of the machines. "Is it possible to change the mold?"

Joji shrugged. "I suppose so. We get different molds for different shoes. If you had a specific kind you wanted to use it probably could be."

Phil nodded. "I have a special kind of mold I'd like to use for a new brand of shoe."

"I thought you sold Tiger shoes."

Phil looked to see if anyone was listening. He leaned toward Joji. "I did. But I'm going to try and make my own shoes. I think I can make better shoes than Tigers."

"And they will have different soles?"

"Yes. Different soles and a different look. I'm going to make shoes that enhance the athlete's performance."

Joji nodded. "I understand. Shoes that run faster."

"Exactly." Phil smiled. "Show me where the sewing is done."

Joji led Phil to the middle of the factory where dozens of large industrial sewing machines operated by intent young women hummed. Phil nodded. "This is very impressive. But we will need to make the machines work on materials other than leather. There are fabrics that are lighter and stretch more."

"What color will you make your shoes?" Joji asked.

Phil thought for a moment. "I don't know. All sorts of colors, I suppose."

Joji motioned for Phil to follow. They made their way to Joji's workstation, where he had a wide variety of different colors of leather sitting in piles at the base of his machine. "People think shoes should only be brown or black. Or if they are athletic shoes, they should be white or gray. But what if shoes could be many different colors? New colors for a new kind of shoe."

Phil picked up some of the leather pieces Joji had pressed out of his machine. He rolled the leather back and forth in his hands. He picked up different colors and put them next to each other. After a few minutes he turned to Joji. "I like different colored shoes. They could be distinctive."

Joji picked up white, black, and red pieces of leather and put them next to each other. "Wouldn't this make a nice combination?"

Phil studied them for a moment. "Those colors belong on bas-ketball shoes." He pointed to a combination of yellow and blue. "And those could be running shoes." He folded his arms. "You know the one thing that's missing?"

Joji shook his head.

"A logo. Something that goes on the shoes themselves. Adidas has the three stripes. Puma has that weird arch shape. Even Tigers have some stripes across them. I don't want stripes, but I need something. Something that will go across the side of the shoe and make it clear what kind of shoe it is. I hired an expensive advertising firm to figure it out. They keep coming up with different shapes, but none of them look good on the side of a shoe."

Joji looked at the floor. Scattered about were several scraps of leather in various shapes. He picked up one that looked like a rolling wave. "What about this? Your shoes could have a wave on them."

Phil put the wave on the side of his own shoe. He moved it up and down. He moved it forward and backward. Finally, he flipped it over. "It looks like a swoosh," he said.

Joji nodded. "Yes, a swoosh."

"I like it," Phil said after staring at it for a few more minutes. "I like the swoosh."

Joji picked up the piece of leather and handed it to Phil. "Keep it as a souvenir. Something to remember." He bowed.

Phil bowed.

Sara and Jane sat down directly across the restaurant table from Ian. "We think we've found it."

Ian looked up from his miso soup. "Found what?"

"The source material." Sara's eyes grew bright as she spoke.

"Source for your lyrics?"

Jane nodded. "Yes. We found a great source. Completely out of the blue."

"All right then. Let's see it."

Sara held up a book. Ian looked at it and took it from her. He read the title. "*Underground Poetry: Words of the World's Greatest Revolutionaries.*" He opened it and began to turn the pages. "Looks like you've got some bits here."

Sara clapped her hands. "It's totally who we are. Artistic anachronisms."

Jane added, "It's like our artistic expression is a means of showing how differently we see the world, yet we are indifferent to how the world sees us."

Ian nodded slowly. "Interesting. You're using the art of others to express how little you're about the influence others have on your art."

"And we found some good material. Including some from Japan."

Ian flipped through the book. "Have you chosen one?"

"We have a few in mind."

"Well, bloody all right then. Show me what you've got when you put something together."

―――――――

A year later Joji was working on a rice farm in Toyama Prefecture when the farmer informed him there was a call from his mother. He went to the farmhouse and picked up the phone.

His mother's voice sounded excited and surprised. "Joji, there is a letter for you from America. Have you been to America recently?"

"No. I haven't gone to America."

"It has a bank number and says a fund has been set up for you. A fund with money."

"I don't know why anyone would set up a bank fund for me," Joji responded.

Joji's mother cleared her throat. "It says it's payment for a souvenir. From someone called Phillip." There was silence on the phone as Joji's mother waited for a response. Hearing none she cleared her throat. "Have you been selling souvenirs?"

"No, Mother. It was just something I gave to a man when I was making shoes."

"Well, it must have been very valuable. You probably shouldn't have given it to him. I can only imagine what it's worth since he set up this fund for you."

"I don't think it was that valuable. It was just a bit of leather."

Joji's mother sighed. "I'm certain it was more than a bit of leather. You should be more careful what you give to people. You might be giving away a fortune and don't know it."

"It really was just a piece of leather."

Joji's mother let out a disapproving sigh. "It can't be taken back now. But at least you've got some money to your name. Quite a lot of money. You certainly have enough to come home and see your parents. Just try not to be so blind about giving away valuables next time."

"Just a piece of leather."

―――――――

Several years after Phil visited the factory and set up Joji's fund,

Joji visited the factory where he had briefly been employed. All the machines and materials used to manufacture shoes were gone and replaced with industrial scale computer chip manufacturing tools. People who had once engaged in cutting and sewing now wore clean suits with face masks and gloves. Much of the old factory had been upgraded with painted white floors, bright lights, and good ventilation. The managers didn't wear ties and wandered around among the workers.

Joji stopped outside the gate of the factory and noticed a large post that had once indicated where workers needed to go before they started their shifts. On the post he wrote:

> *Gray factory floor*
> *Colorful, friendly shoes makes*
> *The perfect guest*

At the bottom of the haiku after his name he made a small mark that art critics argue over incessantly. Was it some added bit of Kanji that might reveal Jo Ojisan's identity? Or was it the mark of a word the great poet was considering but then did not complete? As they quarreled the average person might note that simply by looking at their feet, they might notice a modest similarity between the mark and the shape sewn into the side of their Nike sneakers.

CHAPTER 10

Sapporo

Long night wintertime
A good, happy house mourns
because of the father

—Jo Ojisan

It was clear to Sy and the members of Uncle Joe's Band that Stygian Teal was gradually becoming comfortable playing in larger venues to a foreign audience. Allison still introduced the group, but at the end of the set Jane or one of the other members of the group would say something in Japanese, to the delight of the crowd.

A day after their third show, the members of Uncle Joe's Band were sitting in a Sushi bar. The bar was tiny, with just enough room for the bar, a half dozen barstools, and a counter for the sushi chef on the other side.

When Jane burst through the door Rod had put a piece of tuna sashimi in his mouth with a large dollop of wasabi. He immediately started to sneeze and then grabbed a cup of water and quickly downed it, eyes watering from the wasabi.

"We've got it," Jane said. "We've got a new song. And it's totally dope."

Rick leaned toward Steve. "Dope is good, right?"

Steve nodded.

Ian set down his teacup. "Well, that's wonderful. I can't wait to hear it."

"How about now?" Steve added.

The enthusiasm on Jane's face waned a bit. "I'm not sure it's ready to perform. We just have the lyrics and a bit of a tune."

"Works for me," Rick said as he slurped some tea.

Rod patted the seat beside him. "Yes, let's hear," he said, his voice strained from wasabi.

Jane sat next to Rod and put a notebook on the bar. She started to sing,

> *Bring down the mountain*
> *Bring down the noise*
>
> *Time to make a new beginning*
> *Time to make a choice*
>
> *We are in this together, all aboard our ark*
> *Sailing through the stormy seas*
> *Blind and in the dark.*

Rick held up his hand. "I don't get it. You're on a mountain yelling something, but then you got on board a ship?"

Steve tilted his head. "I thought it was an ark. Is that different from a ship?"

Rod rolled his eyes. "Duh, it's an ark. Like Noah's Ark, with all the animals."

Rick nodded. "Right. So, the singer is on a mountain yelling to get on Noah's ark?"

Ian looked at Jane. "You should ignore them. They are bloody ignoramuses."

Jane smiled. "I was." She looked at Rick. "To be clear, the mountain is a metaphor for all the environmental problems we suffer." She turned to Steve. "And the Ark, like Noah's Ark, is the earth, the only place we all have to live."

Ian tapped his chopsticks on the sushi tray. "Quite right. We are all on a giant ark called earth, hurtling through space and time, utterly reliant on each other. And we must make a choice about how we treat each other and this place we live."

"Oh, now I see it," Rod replied, picking up a piece of sashimi.

"And?" Jane looked at each of Uncle Joe's Band's members. "What do you think? Does it sound okay?"

"I think it does," Steve replied. "I think you just have to add some sound to the lyrics and you may have something."

Jane frowned. "We already have the sound."

"Have you actually played the song?" Rod asked, more directly.

"We have. Sort of." Jane hesitated. "We played it a couple times. It's still in development."

Ian set down his chopsticks. "You should go practice. Everything will be at our venue in Sapporo on Wednesday. Check with Sy. I bet she'll want you to play it."

Rod tapped the paper the lyrics were written on. "Where did you find the inspiration?"

Jane smirked. "Want to borrow it?"

"No, I'm just curious."

"I'll get back to you on that one." Jane stood, put the page of lyrics in her pocket, and left. The men watched her walk back across the street, curious and bemused.

Steve cleared his throat. "She's got to be the one. It's not normal to be that excited about lyrics. Has to be a heritable trait."

Rick waved at the sushi shop's proprietor. He held up a credit card, which the sushi chef took and began preparing the bill. "At some point you're going to have to confront the issue. Have you thought about how you're going to do that?"

Ian tapped his fingers on the counter. "Yes. I just don't know when and how. It's confusing, really. I can't confirm that Jane's my daughter, but we've sort of assumed she is. And yet the other girls seem equally as likely if you consider the matter objectively."

The room was silent for a moment. Rod cleared his throat. "Well, think about how we dealt with Allison. All that mumbling and bumbling, until we finally just came out and asked the question."

Ian grimaced. "Yes, but you'll recall she didn't know the answer right away."

The sushi chef handed Rick the bill, which he signed and handed back. He stood and looked at Ian. "You're going to have to address it. How and when is ultimately up to you."

Rod stood and stretched. "There's another consideration. How will they react when they find out why we chose to bring them on tour?"

Steve shook his head. "I'm not worried. They're having a great time, and they're good. They're really good. Sy wouldn't have had them along unless they could hold their own. And they are."

The others nodded.

———

Three shows in Kobe were followed by a day of rest and then a day traveling to Sapporo.

Throughout the stay in Kobe, Allison had spent little time with the band, trying instead to prove her worth as a roadie. She would meet with Rod around midday, but otherwise spent her time dragging crates and equipment from set to set, taping cords to the stage floor, checking amplifier ranges, and trying to prove she belonged to the stage crew as much as any of the others, mostly men, who did the same thing.

After arriving in Sapporo, Allison and Rod took a walk through the center of the city, an area filled with markets and restaurants.

"Is Ian going to ask Jane?" Allison asked.

"I think he wants to ask her. He's just afraid to."

Allison looked in the window of a Daiso shop. "I don't think I told you I took band class this year."

"You mean in school?"

"Yeah. I play percussion."

Rod chuckled. "You mean you play the drums?"

"Yeah. All kinds of drums. Everything from the kettle-drum to the triangle."

"Did you want to play the drums?"

Allison folded her arms. "No, but our band doesn't include guitar, so I was stuck with the drums."

Rod pointed to a teapot with several kanjis and a picture of a pink cat on it. "You should get that for your grandparents."

Allison shook her head. "No, they don't drink tea."

Rod nodded. "Okay. Well, you should find them something. How are they doing?"

"Pretty good. Grandpa had surgery six months ago. Grandma and I took care of him for about six weeks. He got better, but I had to miss school for a couple weeks."

Rod thought for a moment. "Why didn't you call me? We could have found someone to help. I don't like the idea of you missing school."

Allison unfolded her arms and put her hands in the pockets of her leather jacket. "I know, but I had to. Gramps couldn't even get out of bed."

Rod put his arm around her shoulders. "I know, I'm just saying, next time let me know. I can help." He paused for a moment before continuing. "Where was your mother in all this? Did she help at all?"

Allison looked sideways. "Of course not. She wasn't anywhere to be found. I haven't seen her since before Grandpa got sick."

Rod sighed. He could feel Allison stiffen when he mentioned her mother. Still not entirely certain where or when Allison had been conceived, he wasn't entirely certain he remembered her mother, though when confronted about it, Allison had made it very clear her mother had pinpointed Rod as her father.

Despite Allison's assurance, Rod asked for a paternity test to ensure he was her father. Though Allison had at first resisted the idea, she too decided that certainty was important and agreed to the test.

The day the test arrived, Allison and the other members of Uncle Joe's Band gathered in their dilapidated Vallejo house and held their collective breath. Though the results weren't a surprise there had been a combination of disappointment and relief all around.

After the test Rod's paternal role took time to establish. As much as he had wanted to be Allison's father, he knew that the lack of his presence earlier in her life would lead to a certain dissonance that would take time to overcome. He was careful not to reach out to her mother or grandparents, with whom she lived, until Allison deemed it appropriate. Even then he was careful to conform to whatever would make her most comfortable. Slowly, over time, trust was built and they developed some semblance of a parent-child relationship.

"Does your mother even know you're in Japan?" Rod asked.

"I texted her. But who knows if she read it?"

"Well, your grandparents are aware. Right?" Rod raised an eyebrow.

"Yes. They are both aware. I left them all my contact information and told Sy to call them if anything bad happened."

Rod smiled. "Okay then. I just want to make sure someone knows. You know in case something happens."

Allison pointed to a small pink purse. "I should get one of those for Grandma. She keeps her coins in one of those." She walked into the store with Rod following close behind. She picked up the purse and walked up to the counter where a clerk dressed in pink scanned a barcode.

Rod handed her a card. "I got it."

Allison smiled.

In April 1998, Joji Kinsura made his way back to Sapporo for his father's funeral. The ososhiki was an elaborate affair that followed the Buddhist tradition of seven days of ceremonies, followed by ceremonies every seventh day until the forty-ninth day.

It would be an exaggeration to suggest that Joji was estranged from his father. He simply hadn't seen him with any regularity over the preceding decade. Aside from the occasional visit to Sapporo or the phone call to his mother, Joji simply hadn't had reason to interact with his father. And in turn his father, who had risen through the ranks of the Sapporo Brewing Company, had little reason to interact with his wayward vagabond son.

Uncertain exactly why Joji had chosen not to follow his father into business, or for that matter any respectable profession, Joji's father had learned to simply accept the idea that Joji might not perceive the world in the same way he did. Years of trying to get Joji to acclimate to a life of hard work, privilege, and sacrifice in the name of achieving an upper-class salary left Joji's father disappointed and finally resigned that Joji would never follow a life similar to his father. Once a detente had been established it became easier for father and son to interact both on family occasions as well as those instances whereupon the rest of Joji's family came together.

Despite its name the headquarters of the Sapporo Brewing Company had long since left Sapporo for the much more business-friendly environs of Tokyo. All that was left on Hokkaido, the northernmost island in the Japanese archipelago, was a museum and small brewery. As other executives left Sapporo, Joji's father rose in the local ranks until he became the head of the local Sapporo operations.

Among the elites in Sapporo, the death of the head of the largest local business, synonymous with the name of the city, left a wake of adulation and outpouring of sympathy when Joji's father died. Joji's boyhood home was beset by a never-ending stream of mourners, each clad in black bearing a gift or card for his mother.

When Joji arrived home, a day after his father's passing, he was greeted at the door by an aunt, one he hadn't seen in many years. She looked at him for a moment and then called to Joji's mother, "Did you expect a vagrant?"

Joji heard his mother respond, "No, is he from the monastery?"

Much to his aunt's surprise, Joji took the door handle from his aunt and stepped past her into the house. Little had changed since he had seen it a few years earlier. Designed to appear luxurious, and accommodate large social gatherings, the combination of faux marble floors, crystalline light fixtures and sconces placed to accentuate the height of the ceilings, it remained the cold and sterile environment Joji had come to avoid.

When Joji's aunt started to protest, Joji simply ignored her and waited until he saw his mother marching down the hall. She wore a black kimono with dark blue obi (sash). When she saw Joji she stopped and held up a hand toward his aunt. "Oh, it's just Joji." She gave Joji a hug and then brushed off her clothes. "It's about time you got here. I've had so much to do and had to do it on my own." She pointed toward the kitchen. "Put yourself to work."

In the kitchen Joji found a small army of elderly women, all loudly shouting instructions at each other while carefully processing enough food to fill the orders at a moderately sized restaurant. One of the women looked up, saw Joji, and with little fanfare pointed toward a tray of vegetable gyoza, edamame, and chilled tofu. "Take those to the dining room," she directed. "And clean yourself up."

Joji picked up the tray and made his way to the dining room amidst several middle-aged men in black suits and women in dark dresses. They spoke quietly in small groups. None acknowledged Joji as he entered the room. As he set the tray down, he saw his mother. "What are you doing?" she said loudly.

"Putting myself to work," Joji responded.

"Mingle with our guests." She pointed at the tray. "Other people can do that."

Joji nodded. He looked around the room. Not recognizing anyone, he approached a small group of well-dressed guests. He bowed. "Hello. I'm Joji Kinsara. Thank you for coming to honor my father."

One of the men in the group responded. "We are sorry for your loss. Your father was a great man."

Joji thanked the man, bowed again, and couldn't think of anything else to say. He moved on to another small group of well-heeled mourners. And then another. For the rest of the day he seemed to do little else. Finally at a late hour his mother began to move everyone out of the house. For the first time Joji saw his mother smile. She looked smaller than he remembered.

As a few of the women in the kitchen picked up dishes and began to clean, Joji's mother sat in the kitchen at a small table. She motioned for Joji to sit next to her.

"Thank you for coming," she said as she put her hand on his arm. "I know you and your father didn't see the world in the same way, but he still missed you."

Joji suddenly felt a great sadness. "I missed him. We never understood each other, but we were at peace. I wasn't the son he wanted, but he let me be who I am. Most fathers wouldn't have accepted me."

"I think he envied you, in a way. Most of us become what we are expected to be, whether we were supposed to be that way. You became who you wanted, regardless of everyone else. It is a great thing to be that way. Very rare."

Joji nodded.

"Do you know what he liked to do most? The thing he loved above all else was painting. He loved to paint. Watercolors were his favorite."

Joji looked sideways at his mother. "Why didn't he ever become a painter?"

"Because his father never would have allowed it."

Joji and his mother sat silently for a few more moments. The women in the kitchen were beginning to leave, each waving to Joji's mother as they left.

After a time, Joji's mother stood and made her way off to bed, while Joji sat alone in the kitchen contemplating the life his father led and how he had accepted Joji, despite their apparent differences.

Days after Joji arrived home and the funeral services for his father were completed, he and his mother were to attend a reception in honor of Joji's father. Joji's mother insisted he wear a dark suit with a white shirt and blue tie. The starched collar itched and the pants seemed too tight, but Joji assented to his mother's demand.

The reception was held in the new Sapporo Brewery Museum and was to be attended by all the upper management of the company, several local officials including the mayor of Sapporo. The museum had been created within an old brick brewery from the Meiji period, complete with smokestacks and stained glass. The interior had been rebuilt to include a large beer hall and restaurant as well as a gift shop and the exhibits that made up the museum itself. The reception took place in the beer hall, complete with beer steins and waitresses dressed in traditional German garb. The mood was unusually festive for a funeral reception but seemed appropriate to honor a longstanding member of the Sapporo Beer family.

In the front of the Beer Hall was a large picture of Joji's father along with a list of professional accomplishments, several bottles of beer, and a candle with a large, ornate bowl with incense sticks to be placed on a small altar in front of the picture. Despite the juxtaposition of the German beer hall, altar, and bottles of beer, no one in the room batted an eye or acted as though it was anything out of the ordinary.

Joji bowed before the portrait of his father, lit some incense, and placed it on the altar. He bowed again and turned back toward the rest of the room. As he did, a Japanese waitress, dressed in dirndl, shoved a stein in his hand and said in a cheery voice, "Sapporo lager, senses never forget."

As the waitress turned away a man in a gray suit appeared. He had graying hair and wire rimmed glasses. He shoved his hand into Joji's and shook it. "You must be Joji. I am Kenji Osaka. I was a close friend of your father."

Joji shook the man's hand, noting his soft skin and manicured nails. "It is nice to meet you, Kenji."

"Your father spoke of you often. He called you 'the traveler.'"

Joji's eyes widened. "My father spoke of me often? He had a name for me?"

"Yes. Your travels were very influential in our upcoming marketing campaign."

"Did my travels influence a marketing campaign?"

"Oh yes. In the next few years, we are going to begin advertising in the United States. We are planning on television advertisements that focus on our 'legendary' beer. They will conclude as we offer a prize for someone who purchases our beer. We are calling it our 'legendary journey' prize."

Joji was quiet for a moment, shocked that his father thought of him as something other than a ne'er-do-well who couldn't settle down long enough to hold a job or start a family. "What did he say about my travels?"

"Oh, he said you had traveled far and wide. That you had gone from Sapporo to Okinawa, Tokyo, Kobe, and everywhere in between. He said you were like the wind."

Joji was silent again, stunned.

The man touched Joji's arm. "Where were you most recently? What great adventures did you have? I'm certain you have many wonderful stories."

"I have met many people and seen many things," Joji finally responded. "For the most part, people are all pretty similar. They do the same things, they want the same things, they even feel the same things: We are all much more like each other than any of us would care to admit. And that's the sad part of it: we have to find the little things that are different in order to differentiate ourselves from each other, rather than understanding that, mostly, we are the same."

Kenji stepped back. "That was very wise. You are very much like your father."

Joji excused himself and made his way to the restroom, where he sat and cried for several minutes.

CHAPTER 11

Sukeban

When the girls start singin'
And the crowd hears the noise
They shimmy and shake
And forget about the boys

—Stygian Teal, "Crowd Noise"

Sy stood in front of Stygian Teal, Uncle Joe's Band, and several stage-hands in a conference room at the Sapporo Marriott. "Okay. Practice begins in an hour. You'll have a short period of time for lunch, and then, Uncle Joe, you have a reception with the Sapporo Musical Society. Stygian Teal, you'll be taking a tour of the city. The rest of you have the afternoon off." Sy looked up, not expecting anyone to react to her daily briefing.

"Why are we the ones who have to go to the reception?" Rick whined.

Sy retorted, "You're the marquee. It's a good thing."

Sara raised her hand. "Are there onsens here?"

"There are onsens everywhere in Japan. We can arrange for you to visit one at the end of your tour."

Sara smiled.

One of the roadies raised his hand. "Are there any of those bath houses here?"

Allison leaned forward and whispered, "Those are the onsens Sara asked about."

"Oh. Right." The roadie nodded as though he had known all along.

Sy sighed. "Okay. We're done here. There's a bus outside to take you to practice." She pointed at the conference room door.

On the bus Allison sat next to Rod. "Can I come with you to the reception?" she asked.

"I don't know why not. Will you have all your other duties completed?"

"Yes, sir."

Rod looked at her. "Why are you interested in the reception?"

"I read in *Lonely Planet* that the Japanese are big on ceremonies. They have welcome ceremonies, goodbye ceremonies, friendship ceremonies, work ceremonies, and on and on. I just thought I should experience one while I'm here."

Rod raised his eyebrows. "You read that in *Lonely Planet*?"

Allison nodded.

"All right then. You can come to the Sapporo Musical Society reception."

Before Joji left Sapporo he stopped his van near Odori Park. The great Sapporo Snow Festival was scheduled to begin the following day and Joji wanted to walk among the snow and ice statues being created by artisans along the thoroughfare in the middle of the park. He made his way past snow sculptures of the Eiffel Tower, the White House, and several anime characters when he found an empty space with a very large piece of ice. It appeared as though someone had planned to create a statue and then simply left, opting instead to work on a snow sculpture or visiting the local market. Chisels, picks, and a small ladder sat beside the block.

Joji looked up and down the walkway. He stepped closer to the ice and put his hand on it. The block was nearly three meters tall and a meter wide. Large screws attached it to a wooden base. Without thinking Joji picked up a chisel and tapped it on the ice. A few chips fell to the ground. He put his finger over the groove the chisel had created. With a bit more vigor he struck the block of ice again and more shards fell to the ground. He began to set the chisel down, but after looking up and down the street and seeing no one, he struck the block again. And again. After a few minutes he set the ladder against the block and climbed up near its top. A bit more diligently he began to chisel and scratch, slowly cutting into the ice, seeing in his mind the shape of letters already marked within the great block simply waiting to be excised. For hours he toiled. By the time he had finished and stepped away from the great block of ice his hands hurt from the cold. But his mind and spirit felt relieved, as though some part of him had reconciled his past and future. He set the chisel and hammer on the ground next to the block of ice and walked back to his van.

———————

As the Snow Festival judges made their way through Odori Park, they noticed a large crowd gathered around one particular statue. It wasn't unusual for an international team to produce a crowd-pleasing rendition of a cartoon character or political figure. Tourists and locals might gather round taking selfies or commenting on the sculpture even as the judges assessed whether it should win.

As they approached the crowd it became clear this wasn't simply a snow or ice statue. A tall block of ice sat behind a fence with kanjis carved into it. As the judges pushed their way through the onlookers, they wondered what could possibly be so special about the block of ice with a few letters chiseled into its surface. Voices in the crowd murmured, "Jo Ojisan."

———————

The Sapporo Musical Society reception was held in the Sapporo Concert Hall Gallery, immediately adjacent to the hall itself. Chandeliers hung from ornate ceilings over a blue and gold carpet, creating a sense of grandeur and opulence that might normally befit a more ostentatious venue.

As Uncle Joe's Band entered, they were greeted with a smattering of applause from a very well-heeled crowd. Men in suits and women in dresses appeared as though they'd planned on attending a matinee performance of Rigoletto, rather than a reception for a moderately successful metal band. A few of the men in the crowd approached the band, shook hands with the members and took selfies. A gray-haired man in a gray suit suddenly appeared, stood in front of the band and bowed. He began to speak in Japanese. The band nodded as though they understood. Finally, a young woman began to translate. "He says the Sapporo Musical Society welcomes you and can't wait to see you sing."

Ian bowed to the man. "Tell him we are honored to be here."

Rick whispered to Rod, "What does he mean about seeing us sing?"

"I'm sure he's talking about the show," Rod replied.

After a bit more shaking hands and bowing, the band was escorted to seats at the front of the room near a small dais where a microphone and stand stood. As the rest of the crowd took their seats the man with the gray hair stood atop the dais and began to speak, in Japanese, again. Several times he motioned toward the band and received a smattering of applause from the crowd. As he spoke the bandmates looked at one another, not quite sure how to respond.

After he was done speaking, the man in the gray suit bowed and stepped off the dais. As he did, a younger man, dressed casually wearing jeans and a sport coat, took his place. He began to speak and, much to the band's relief, alternated between Japanese and broken English. "It is a great honor to welcome the American rock and roll group to Sapporo. We are excited to hear them sing. Their music captures the excitement and enthusiasm of America. I am the mayor of Sapporo. Welcome." He continued speaking in Japanese for another several minutes, without translation.

When the mayor finished speaking another gentleman stepped up on the dais, spoke briefly, then another and then another. For nearly an hour speaker after speaker rose, spoke, gestured toward the band, bowed, and receded back to the crowd. Finally, a young woman stepped to the microphone and spoke in English, "Thank you, Uncle Joe's Band, for coming to Sapporo. Welcome to the Sapporo Musical Society. We can't wait to hear you sing." Unlike the other speakers, when she finished, she stepped off the dais, bowed in front of the band, and motioned for them to take the stage.

The band-mates looked at Ian, who nodded and stepped up to the mike. "Bloody great to meet you all. We've always wanted to come to Sapporo and are overwhelmed by your hospitality." He bowed and began to step off the dais. A murmur rippled through the crowd.

"I think you said something wrong," Rod whispered loudly.

Ian shrugged. The rest of the band rose, turned toward the crowd, and waved. A disquieting silence followed.

The young woman who had preceded Ian on the dais stepped forward. "Are you going to sing?" she asked.

Rick nodded. "Yes. Tonight, at our show."

Steve leaned toward Ian. "I think they want us to sing something. Now."

"What the bloody hell am I supposed to sing?" Ian replied.

"Just sing something. Fast."

Rick turned toward Ian. "Just throw out some of those high-pitched notes from 'The Green Aardvark.'"

The crowd continued to grumble and heads continued to shake as the band huddled, trying to decide what to do.

"Dude, get up there." Rod grabbed Ian's arm.

"You bloody get up there," Ian replied, pulling his arm away. "And don't put your mitts on me, mate."

"Screw you, man. You're the singer, they want a song, so freakin' sing," Rod replied, pushing Ian in the chest.

The crowd, beginning to appreciate the dissension among the band-mates, quieted.

"He's right. You wanted to be the singer, so get your ass up there and sing," Steve said, turning Ian around and pushing him toward the dais.

Ian, glasses askew, twisted back toward Steve, throwing his right fist toward Steve's jaw. When the fist landed Steve's jaw remained unmoved. Ian pulled his hand back, cursing from the pain. Rick stepped forward to try and separate Steve and Ian, but tripped over the microphone cord and fell onto the dais. Before Steve could respond to Ian's punch, Rod grabbed him by the shoulders and pulled him away from Ian. Ian, stepping backwards, began to trip on the dais, but grabbed the microphone stand and was able to keep himself from falling.

As Steve struggled to pull himself free from Rod's grip, Ian reached up and pulled the mike from its stand. "Bloody fine," he muttered.

The seriousness of the Nippon News Network anchors was invariably unflinching. Without a hint of emotion, night after night, they delivered the news. Tragic events were reported dry eyed. Human interest stories were read without the hint of a smile. It was this unerring consistency that might explain why viewers long remembered Tashiro Kyoko's unapologetic laughter when reporting on an event at the Sapporo Musical Society.

The report started innocently enough. "The Sapporo Musical Society hosted a reception for the American heavy metal band, Uncle Joe's Band, today. The society often hosts famous musical guests who visit the region. Following a series of speeches, a scuffle broke out, not between members of the Society, but between members of Uncle Joe's Band."

As she spoke, cell phone images of Ian punching Steve and the subsequent melee flashed across the screen.

"The fight was finally broken up, not by security, but by a sixteen-year-old girl."

Images were shown of Allison stepping in between Steve and Ian, yelling at both, and wagging her finger. As if by force of personality, she pointed at Steve, who immediately sat down. She pointed at Rod, who dusted off Steve's jacket as though he hadn't been clutching it a moment before. She told Rick to stand up.

"Clearly this young woman knows how to stop a fight."

Ian had the microphone and Allison pointed at him. He stood on the dais for a moment before letting out a very loud scale that rose to a heightened crescendo before falling back to nearly a whisper.

"And this was the singer from Uncle Joe's Band, which is clearly run by the young woman. Many commentators have taken to calling her Power Girl. Perhaps we will see Power Girl again at the upcoming concert."

"What did you do?" Sy's arms were crossed, her brow furrowed, and her complexion dark. "That was supposed to be a nice, quiet reception with the city elites."

"He started it!" Ian pointed at Steve.

"Our singer wouldn't sing. It was embarrassing," Steve replied. "I just gave him a little push."

"He knocked me into the stage!" Ian shot back. He pointed at Rick and Rod. "You saw him!"

"Didn't mean to knock you back into the stage. I wanted you to get up there and do your job!"

"Shut up!" Sy held up her hand. "I'm going to have to figure out how to spin this into something less awful than what it is. And since you two can't keep your composure, you are going to make up." She looked at both. "Now. Make up now."

Steve looked at Ian. "Sorry."

Ian held out his hand. "It's all right, mate. I should have just belted something out and been done with it."

Sy stepped back. "Okay then." As she did Stygian Teal entered the hotel lobby, where Sy had been meeting with Uncle Joe's Band.

Allison felt Sara's shirt. "This is amazing. Where did you get it?"

"The onsen we went to today. They have these clothes made from bamboo fibers. They're super soft."

Indira blurted out, "And the onsen was the best one yet. They have these scrubs you put on and they make your skin super soft."

Sy gave a loud "humph," turned and walked away.

Allison touched Indira's hand. "Wow. That is soft. I should have gone with you guys."

Jane smiled. "Really? Then you wouldn't be famous."

"What do you mean?"

Kara tapped on her phone and handed it to Allison. "You've gone viral."

Allison stared at the screen for a moment. "The incident at the Musical Society went viral?"

Kara smiled. "Not just that. It's you. You're what they're talking about."

"What are they saying?" Rod asked.

"They keep calling me Sukeban," Allison replied.

Rod raised his eyebrows. "What is sukeban?"

"It means girl boss," Indira replied, nudging Allison.

Rick pointed at Ian and Steve. "You made her a girl boss."

Jane shook her head. "It's a bit more complicated than that. Sukeban also means delinquent. It was a name they gave to girl gang members. They were like the girl mafia."

Rod frowned. "They're saying my daughter is a delinquent?"

Jane lowered her voice. "Or she's in the mafia. I'm surprised you didn't know."

Steve pointed at Rod. "She's in the mafia. Maybe she could do something about that critic at *Rolling Stone*. You know, he could wake up next to a horse's head or something."

Rod growled. "She's not in the mafia."

Steve shrugged. "How would you know?"

"Because I'm her father. If she were in the mafia, I'd be in the mafia."

Jane patted Rod on the shoulder. "It's the girl mafia. So maybe not."

Allison put up both her hands. "Okay, stop. I'm not in the mafia, I'm not a delinquent, and I'm not a subu... whatever you call it. I'm the referee of a rather sorry bunch who can't seem to figure out how to behave in public, who seem to think that acting like children is acceptable in polite society. I am the teen who is parenting the parents, making certain they don't screw things up so badly, they don't ruin their lives and careers."

The room was silent.

Finally, Jane interjected. "Yeah, that's great but girl mafia sounds way cooler. I'd go with that."

Rod nodded. "Yes, I think I'd actually prefer the girl mafia over that parenting the parent stuff."

Steve put his arm around Allison. "Right. And understand, we don't think less of you for being in the girl mafia, whatever that is. We think more."

Allison rolled her eyes and looked at Sy. "Are you sure I'm not old enough to drink in Japan?"

The crowd at the concert in Sapporo was poite while Stygian Teal played their first set. After the first few songs they politely clapped. A few stood up and danced. During the second set the chants began. Jane pretended not to hear them at first, carrying on with the next song and then the next. By the time she reached the third song in her second set the chants couldn't be ignored. Jane paused and looked offstage. She pointed at Allison. Allison shook her head. Jane looked back at the crowd. "Subekan?" she said into the microphone while raising her arms.

The crowd roared.

Jane waved at Allison again. Allison shook her head and didn't budge. Jane stepped offstage.

"They want you."

"I'm not going out there," Allison replied.

"Why not?"

"What am I supposed to do? Yell and pretend I'm in charge?"

"Yes. That would be perfect."

Allison rolled her eyes.

Sy appeared, seemingly out of nowhere. She tapped Allison's shoulder. "Just go out and wave. That's all you have to do."

Allison rolled her eyes again. "Fine." She stepped past Jane and walked on stage. The crowd roared.

CHAPTER 12

Okinawa

Late beach lobster
A good, friendly soldier drinks
In a loud uniform

—Jo Ojisan

It wasn't until the late 1990s that Joji's Subaru van made it to Okinawa. The island's tropical climate and western breezes allowed him to sleep on the roof of his van each night, watching the stars and the moon. Even when a tropical storm struck and rivers of water poured from the sky, Joji found the island warm and inviting.

Getting to Okinawa had proven complicated, less so for Joji than for his van. The only ferries from the mainland took over a day, were beyond his budget, and didn't carry cars. Still, he found a small freighter being loaded with cargo containers. As the containers were being loaded, he drove the van into one that was only half full of crates of breakfast cereal, closed the door, and waited to be hoisted onto the ship.

When he arrived in Okinawa, Joji's container was taken off the ship and placed on a truck, which promptly drove to a warehouse on the western corner of the island. When the container was opened the warehouse workers found Joji, his van, and several empty cereal boxes.

After leaving the warehouse, Joji drove south through Naga City. He passed by rice fields, palm trees, small villages, and several convoys of military vehicles. North of Naha City he stopped, found a beach, and went wading in the surf.

He stayed on the beach for two more days, before driving a bit further, finding a camping site near some large rocks. Ever a swimmer,

Joji made his way along the rocks until he noticed a brown claw jutting out from under a rock. He stuck a stick next to the claw and brushed it once, and then again. On the second pass the claw almost instinctively grabbed the stick and Joji pulled a medium-sized lobster from under the rocky ledge. He tossed the gnarled creature onto the beach.

A bit further he found another lobster, then another. Soon a small pile of lobsters rested on the sand, not far from his van.

By evening Joji had built a small fire and pulled out a large wok from somewhere under the passenger's seat. He filled it with seawater, put a lobster in the middle of it, and set it on the fire. After twenty minutes or so he reclaimed the wok and carefully removed the lobster from the boiling seawater. As he sat, chopsticks in hand, cracking open one of the claws, he heard a loud voice speaking in English. "Hot damn!"

Joji turned to see three American men walking toward him. The tallest was bare chested, wore green military issue pants and boots. The shortest wore a red T-shirt emblazoned with "Marines" in yellow. The third had khaki shorts and a green hoodie. They were tall, with close-cropped hair. One wore a baseball cap. They looked like they had been walking for some time.

One of the men pointed at the lobsters. "These yours?" He looked at his friends and flashed a devilish smile.

"Them's some nice bugs, aren't they?" he said, nodding.

Joji, who had been sitting, looked up at him. "They are lobsters."

The men looked surprised. The bare-chested man smiled. "Yup. Them's lobsters. You get them 'round here?"

Joji nodded. "Yes. I got them in the rocks, right over there." He pointed toward the rocky shelf.

One of the men smiled. "Any reason we can't go find some over there?"

Joji shook his head. "No, there should be more. Look for their claws in the surf."

One of the men tipped his hat. "Much obliged."

For the next hour the three men walked along the rocky shore, occasionally sticking their hand into the surf before quickly pulling it out, always empty. Joji watched with some interest as they gradually became more frustrated. After washing out his wok and putting the remaining lobsters in a cooler in his van he made his way to the rocks.

He called out to the men. "Would you like some help?"

One of the men shrugged and pointed to the rocks. "We can't get them out."

Joji found a stick and walked into the surf. "You let them grab the stick." He walked along the edge of the rocks until he found the antenna and a claw jutting out from behind a bit of stone. As the men watched he pushed the stick in front of the claw and moved it back and forth. As the claw closed around the stick, he pulled it forward and up, out of the surf. Before the lobster could release its grip on the stick Joji grabbed the back of its carapace. He lifted it up so the men could see.

An hour later the three Americans and Joji had a small pile of lobsters sitting on the sand next to Joji's van. The Americans looked very excited.

One of the men looked at the pile of lobsters. "The boys at the base are going to love this. Gunna have a crab feed."

"They're lobsters," another replied.

"Yeah, but lobsters are kind of like crabs."

Joji pointed to the lobsters. "Will you take them with you?"

"I got some beers back on the base."

"Ain't no way to get all them bugs back to the crib."

Joji pointed to his van. "I can take you."

The men looked at each other. The man in the hoodie smiled. "That would be great. By the way, what's your name?"

"My name is Joji."

"Nice meetin' you, Joji. I'm Clem, this here's Rails and that's Joe. We're stationed at Camp Courtney." Clem pointed north. "We were walking around the area and kind of got lost."

"No problem. I will find your camp," Joji offered.

The Americans helped Joji load the dozen or so lobsters into the van. They jumped in and Joji began driving toward the American Marine base.

"I.D.s" the guard at the security gate demanded when Joji's van stopped at the entrance to the base. The Marines handed their cards to the guard who quickly scanned them and handed them back to the Americans. He looked at Joji. "I-D."

Joji looked at the Americans. Rails waved his hand. "He's with us. He's a visitor."

"No visitors except for family," the guard replied.

Joe pushed back the brim of his baseball cap. "Well, Private, it turns out he's my cousin." He turned to Joji. "Ain't that right, cuz?"

Joji nodded. "Yes. Cousins."

The guard looked at Joji and then looked at Joe. He shrugged. "Very well. Your cousin will need to sign in at the visitors' center." He waved his hand to allow the van to pass.

Joji drove slowly through Camp Courtney. Small beige-colored buildings were interspersed with large beige-colored buildings. Several grassy fields, with areas well worn by marching and drilling, sat adjacent to each grouping of buildings. At one end of the base was a row of three-story buildings (also beige). Joji followed the three Americans into one of the buildings. After finding it mostly vacant the three Marines and Joji made their way to a grassy space behind the building where several young men were lounging about throwing a football back and forth. A case of beer sat on a wooden table with several empty cans sitting next to it.

As they walked onto the lawn Clem raised a lobster in each hand. "Check this out, gentlemen. We got ourselves a crab feed."

"Clem, they're lobsters," Joe said as he rolled his eyes.

Back slaps and high-fives were followed by someone bringing a large metal pot filled with water and setting it on a barbecue pit next to the wooden table. Soon the water was boiling and the lobsters cooked. In the process Joji (introduced and referred to as Joe's cousin) had a warm beer shoved in his hand and a somewhat worn beige baseball cap stuck on his head.

The revelry continued as the evening wore on. At one-point Joji asked Clem where he might find a restroom. Clem pointed toward a door in one of the buildings.

When Joji returned a few minutes later the men were gone. Empty beer cans and bits of lobster were scattered about the lawn. The coals on the barbecue were still red. Not sure where everyone had gone, he strolled toward the front of the building. The street in front was empty, but inside he could hear someone shouting.

As he turned to go back toward the open park, he nearly bumped into a large man in uniform walking the other direction.

"Excuse me," Joji said.

The man stopped. His eyes narrowed as he looked at Joji. "Excuse me what?" he yelled loudly.

"Excuse me for nearly running into you?" Joji responded.

"Excuse me, Sergeant!" the man yelled. "Excuse me, Sergeant!"

Joji gulped. "Excuse me, Sergeant."

The sergeant pointed at Joji's shirt. "Why aren't you at the barrack inspection? Where is your uniform?"

"I don't have one," Joji replied.

"Well, what in the cockamamie good is a soldier without a uniform?" the Sergeant yelled. "Go to the commissary and get yourself a uniform!"

Joji started to protest. The sergeant lowered his face until it was inches away from Joji's. "Looks like I'm goin' to have to take this Marine to get his uniform since he doesn't seem to know he's in the United States Marine Corps!" The Sergeant turned Joji around, pointed toward the door of the barrack, and yelled, "March, Ten-Hup!"

Joji, uncertain what to do, compliantly followed the sergeant's order. He followed the sergeant past several beige buildings, over the marching ground and into the commissary. The sergeant walked to a counter at the front of the shop. The private stood at attention, saluted, looked at Joji, and stepped into a room behind the counter. He returned a moment later with a camouflage green uniform and black boots. He handed them to Joji. "Here, try these on."

Joji looked for a place to change clothes, but he saw none.

"Dadgummit soldier! We haven't got all day! Put on your uniform so we can see if it fits!" the sergeant screamed.

Joji, still not used to being directly yelled at, immediately started to disrobe and put on the uniform. It was a bit baggy but fit as well as could be expected. Joji picked up his clothes and folded them under his arm.

"All righty then. We've got this Marine in a daggum uniform!" the sergeant yelled.

For a moment Joji wondered how anyone could spend so much time yelling without losing their voice, or how someone could make their way through the world speaking in such a singular and loud monotone.

The sergeant pointed Joji back toward the door of the commissary and began marching Joji back to the barracks.

When Joji arrived back at the barracks it was late into the evening. Clem, Rails, and Joji were standing outside the building along with the rest of the men housed there. All stood at attention as the sergeant marched Joji toward the squad. As Joji marched closer the Marines' eyes grew wide. A few smirks began to emerge from otherwise rigid faces. Finally, someone laughed aloud.

The sergeant stopped and turned toward the squad, his face indicating he was clearly not amused. "Which of you daggum jarheads thinks this whole thing is funny!" he screamed.

A few other men started to giggle. The Sergeant grew red in the face. "I SAID WHICH OF YOU DAGGUM JARHEADS THINK THIS IS FUNNY?"

Clem raised his hand. "I do, Sergeant."

"DO YOU FIND ME FUNNY? DO I MAKE YOU LAUGH?"

Clem tried not to smile. "No, Sergeant. It's the *situation* that's funny. I do not find you funny at all. Definitely not funny, Sergeant. Sir!"

The sergeant turned to the rest of the squad, his face slowly reddening. "WHICH OF THE REST OF YOU FIND THIS FUNNY?! I SAID WHO ELSE!"

Several hands rose.

The sergeant turned to one of the other Marines. "SON CAN YOU IN YOUR INFINITE WISDOM TELL ME WHY THIS SOLDIER'S UNIFORM IS SO DAGGUM SILLY? WHAT ABOUT THIS UNIFORM MAKES YOU LAUGH?"

"Nothing about the uniform, Sergeant. There is nothing humorous about the uniform. It is a very serious uniform, Sergeant."

"THAT IS EXCELLENT NEWS, PRIVATE! IT'S GOOD TO KNOW THERE IS NOTHING HUMOROUS ABOUT THIS MAN'S UNIFORM!"

The sergeant turned back to Clem. "SINCE THIS MAN'S UNIFORM IS SO SERIOUS, WHAT ABOUT THIS SITUATION DO YOU FIND FUNNY?"

Clem cleared his throat. "Well, you see, Sergeant, this man, his name is Joji, this man isn't actually a Marine. Sir."

The sergeant's face turned from dark crimson to bright red. He looked at Joji. He turned and looked at Clem. He looked back at Joji.

"SON, IF YOU ARE NOT A MARINE, WHAT THE DAGNABBIT ARE YOU?"

Joji stood with his back as straight as he could. "I am a poet."

The sergeant's bright red face began to whiten. "A POET. A LA-DE-DA, DR. SUESS, ROBERT FROST POET?"

Joji shook his head. "No. I am a haiku poet."

"A HAY-KOO POET!" The sergeant turned back to the squad. "WHICH OF YOU DAGGUM JAR-HEADS DECIDED IT WAS A GOOD IDEA TO BRING A HAY-KOO POET ONTO THIS BASE?"

Joe, Rails and Clem raised their hands. "We did, Sergeant," Joe replied.

The sergeant's face was now nearly white. "AND WHY DID YOU THINK THIS WAS A GOOD IDEA?"

Rails cleared his throat. "Because he helped catch some lobsters and was helping us cook them. Sir!"

The sergeant closed his eyes. "AND WHICH ONE OF YOU FELT IT WAS A GOOD IDEA TO LET THIS LOBSTER-CATCHING HAY-KOO POET PUT ON THE UNIFORM OF THE UNITED STATES MARINE CORPS!"

Several of the Marines looked at each other. When none responded the sergeant turned toward Clem. "WELL, DADBURNIT, WHICH ONE OF YOU!"

Clem blinked. "You did, sir. You gave the poet a uniform. Sir!"

The sergeant opened his mouth to yell, but when nothing came out, he closed it. Without a word, he turned and walked away.

After Joji had changed back into his clothes and given the uniform back to Clem and returned to his van, the Marines lined up next to it and saluted as he started the engine. Clem handed him the camouflage hat that was a part of the Marine uniform.

"Joji, this is for you. You put on the uniform. It may have been a mistake and you were under duress, but you put it on, nonetheless. Lots of folks refuse to even try. You deserve to keep at least a little piece of it."

Joji put the hat on and saluted. "Thank you, Clem-san. I am honored to have such good friends in the Marines."

Clem saluted one last time. "Semper Fi, Joji. Semper Fi."

CHAPTER 13

The Proposal

Blowy winter
Cherry tree, wise princess marry
near the dragonfly

—Jo Ojisan

After the first show in Sapporo the bands had two days off before the next show. They met for their daily briefing in a corner of the hotel lobby, sprawling about couches and lounge chairs. Sy held a clipboard and stood in the middle of the group.

"Okay. Today we've got a day off. We'll be meeting at the auditorium for practice around two o'clock. Stygian Teal, you'll start and an hour later Uncle Joe's Band you'll be up. Stygian Teal, I suggest you run through some of your new material."

Kara raised her hand. "Can we go to one of the clubs tonight?"

"Absolutely not," Sy said. "We don't go out when we tour. It's troublesome. Always trouble."

Rick chimed in. "Yeah, we've had a few incidents over the years."

"That's an understatement," Sy replied.

Kara raised her hand again. "We aren't going to cause any trouble. We just wanted to check out the local club scene."

Ian turned toward Kara. "First off, there's no need to raise your hand to ask a question. It's just us here. Secondly, you must remember you're a public figure now. When you go out people know who you are. And love, when they know who you are, it's Molly bar the door."

"Yeah, we once had to take out a restraining order," Rick added.

Kara folded her arms. "Really?"

Ian nodded. "Oh yeah. He thought Rick was the reincarnation

of David Bowie. Kept calling him Ziggy and asking if he was going to be headed off into space."

Sy shook her head. "The sad part is Rick doesn't even look like David Bowie."

Rick crossed his arms. "I mean, I think I look a little like him."

Rod patted Rick on the shoulder. "You don't."

"Well, if we can't go out, what should we do?" Jane asked.

"Practice and sleep. It's what you do on tour," Ian replied. "And occasionally perform."

Sy held up her hand. "That is correct, you sleep, eat, practice, and perform. Since there isn't a performance today, we are going to practice." She looked up from her notes in a manner that suggested there wasn't an alternative to her proposal. When silence followed, she continued. "There's one other thing. I want Allison to be a part of the show." She looked at Stygian Teal. "I want you to figure out how to include her in at least one of your sets."

Kara looked at Indira. Indira looked at Jane. Jane looked at Sara, who looked at Sy. "We like Allison, but we aren't going to change who we are to accommodate someone's kid."

Rod stood up. "Hey, I had nothing to do with this."

Sy put down her clipboard. "This isn't a nepotism thing. I'm not asking this because she's Rod's daughter. Allison doesn't even know I'm asking you to do this."

Jane stood. She was nearly six inches taller than Sy. "What is it then? Why do you want us to make Allison part of the band?"

"I didn't say I wanted you to make her part of the band. I just want you to include her in your show. Not for her sake, but for yours." Sy pointed at a newspaper sitting on a coffee table next to the couch that Ian was sitting on. "I've been doing this a long time. Promoting bands. You don't get opportunities like this very often. That sukeban thing has taken off. I inquired about it. It's way more than just a name. It represents a style of clothes, a mindset that isn't that different from the punk movement."

"What the bloody hell are you talking about?" Ian laughed. "Girl boss is a *thing*."

Sy nodded. "It is. You can go look it up. It started back in the 60s. Japan is a rather patriarchal society. The male street gangs wouldn't let girls participate, so some of them formed their own. That morphed into a representation of feminism, violent feminism, at least as I understand it."

Jane folded her arms. "That does sound kind of punk."

Kara raised her hand.

"You don't have to raise your hand," Rod reminded her.

"Check this out." Kara held up her phone. "They have pictures of it." The two bands gathered behind her and stared at the screen.

"They look like they're wearing school uniforms and carrying baseball bats," Rick noted. "It looks kind of creepy."

Steve nodded. "Yeah, like an angry clown."

Jane scratched her head. "I think we can work with this. The schoolgirl uniform thing isn't going to work, but there are elements of what we wear right now we could use to fold this in."

Sy picked up her clipboard. "And get Allison involved. She's the original girl boss. Even if she just introduces you guys. Make her part of the act."

When Stygian Teal took the stage for their second show, the changes in their appearance were subtle. Sara had a streak of blue in her hair. Indira wore a pleated skirt and a leather motorcycle jacket. Jane had a black mark painted under one eye. And during the first set Stygian Teal had added a new guitarist. Allison wore a leather jacket and played along on her green guitar, occasionally joining in the vocals.

In 1992 Joji's van rolled into a secluded area of Tokyo. The area was near Hibiya Park, a wide-open area with plenty of space for walking and relaxing.

As he stepped out of his van, Joji breathed in the warm summer air. The sounds and noise of a bustling Tokyo seemed distant.

As he wandered about the area Joji happened upon a small pond. A paved walking path around the pond was punctuated by several sitting areas, with benches looking across the water. The trees and shrubs were manicured in the Tsukiyama style, complete with a small bridge over a stream running out of the pond.

Joji walked along the path following a dragonfly that seemed to be leading him to something significant. It flitted and dodged up and down, always several feet ahead of Joji, just far enough to be ahead and close enough to be followed.

Halfway around the pond Joji noticed a young woman was sitting on a bench looking out onto the lake. She was dressed in white, with a stylish jacket and shoes. Her hair was pulled into a bun and her necklace of white pearls was so large Joji initially mistook them for golf balls. She appeared upset; her face red as though she had been crying.

Joji cleared his throat. "Are you okay?

She nodded, unconvincingly.

Joji pointed at the seat next to her. "May I sit?"

She nodded again, similarly unconvincingly.

"It is a beautiful garden, isn't it?" Joji said.

"Yes, it is lovely," the woman noted. "I am sorry for my appearance."

"Your appearance is as pleasant as the garden." Joji replied, trying to be positive.

After a moment the woman spoke again. "I am stuck in a dilemma, from which I see no escape. No way out."

Joji nodded. He noticed a piece of paper in the woman's hand. It looked like an invitation, embossed on perfect, clean, white paper. Her clothes appeared expensive, her nails manicured and her hair perfectly coiffed.

"I'm sorry for your dilemma. Is there anything I can do?" Joji asked.

The woman wiped her nose on a handkerchief that appeared from one of her pockets. "No. It is an impossible problem. A man is going to ask me to marry him."

Joji wasn't sure how to respond. After a moment he replied, "Is he a bad man?"

"No, he is a very good one."

"Do you love him?"

"I love him very much." The woman folded her hands and became teary-eyed.

Joji sighed. Clearly the problem was vexing. He wasn't sure what to say next. The dragonfly that he had followed on the walking path landed in front of him on a rock next to the pond. It spread its wings to dry them.

"He is a very powerful, important person and if I marry him my life won't continue as I wanted it to." A tear fell down her cheek. "I will become a symbol, not a person."

"That is a problem," Joji replied. "Does he know of your reticence?"

"He asked me to marry him twice. I said 'no' both times. Today he will ask me again. I cannot keep saying 'no.'"

As she spoke a breeze kicked up across the pond. The water rippled and leaves fell from the trees. The dragonfly stretched its wings and rose from the rock. It floated back across the pond.

"Sometimes the wind changes. Perhaps it is changing now," Joji replied, trying to be hopeful.

The woman said nothing.

Joji decided to try a different approach. "Let me ask you a question. What will make you happy?"

"To be married, to have a family, to be able to serve my country as I was trained to do."

"This man will offer you marriage and a family?"

The woman stopped crying. "Yes."

"Then you only need to figure out the last part. How can you be what you were trained to be?"

The woman tilted her head, considering the possibility.

Joji continued, sensing his words had been helpful. "You should set parameters for your future husband. What you can live with, what you cannot. You can decide how you want to live your life. If he wants to marry you badly enough, he will meet your demands."

The woman dried her eyes. "His life is very constrained. But he is very powerful. If necessary, he can make changes."

"We all have the power to make changes."

The woman nodded. "Yes, we do." She stood and straightened her skirt. "Thank you for your words. My name is Masako. Masako Owada."

"Nice to meet you, Owada Masako. My name is Joji."

Owada Masako bowed and walked away.

Two days later, the Japanese press reported that Crown Prince Hironomiya Naruhito, in line to become the 126th emperor of Japan, was engaged. Masako Owada, a graduate of Harvard and Oxford Universities and a rising star in diplomatic circles, accepted his proposal after rejecting two previous offers. Her rise to the Chrysanthemum Throne was seen as a turning point for the independence of women in Japan. Her daughter and only child, Princess Toshi, is expected to be the first female to ascend to the Imperial Throne.

CHAPTER 14

The Ubiquitous Vending Machine

Sell it fast, sell it cheap
Give me stuff I think I need

—Uncle Joe's Band, "Capitalist Dream"

After Sapporo, the bands prepared to travel south to Fukuoka on the western edge of Japan. Buses and trucks were loaded with stage equipment and drove in a caravan toward the next leg in the tour. Stygian Teal opted to travel separately, taking the shinkansen train from Sapporo to Tokyo and finally to Fukuoka. Allison wanted to travel with her new band, but Sy was clear that she was still part of the road crew and was responsible for loading and unloading equipment. So rather than ride the bullet train she was relegated to the bus with her father and the rest of Uncle Joe's Band.

As was typical for a touring musical act, much of the travel time was spent sleeping, playing mindless games, or staring out the window.

As they boarded the bus, Steve stopped outside the hotel at a row of vending machines. Having no idea how to read the Japanese words under each beverage, he placed his money in the payment slot, closed his eyes and pushed a button. When a bottle fell, he picked it up, opened it, and took a sip. Nodding in approval, he boarded the bus.

An hour or so later the caravan stopped at a rest area along a freeway. The terrain was mountainous with long stretches of tunnels and bridges, and the rest area appeared to have been carved out of the side of one of the mountains.

As the band members stepped off the bus, Steve held the bottle from the vending machine at the hotel. He showed it to Allison. "This stuff is great. I got it randomly from a vending machine at the hotel."

Allison looked at the bottle. "I think it's called milk tea."

"Well, it's great. When we get closer to the city, I'm going to find another vending machine and get some more."

Allison looked around. "Just get one over there." She pointed toward a row of vending machines lined up inside a nook carved into the side of the mountain.

"Wow. I can't believe they put those things all the way out here. Don't mind if I do," he said nonchalantly as he made his way past a bus to the machines.

After the rest stop, Uncle Joe's Band, Allison, and Sy huddled together in the back of the bus.

Allison sat directly in front of Ian. "When are you going to tell them?"

"Tell them what?"

"When are you going to tell them that one of them is your daughter and they are on this tour with you so you can find out?" she replied.

Ian shifted in his seat. "I was going to ask them one at a time. I just haven't had the opportunity."

Rod coughed. "You're afraid."

"Bloody well yes, I'm afraid. What if my daughter gets mad because I wasn't there? Or tells me she hates me? Or something awful like that. Of course, I'm terrified."

Sy sighed. "If it were up to me, you'd wait until the tour was over. But it probably isn't fair to the girls. You need to hurry up and tell them."

Ian shifted in his seat again. "I suppose I must. I'll just have to buck up and do it."

As they spoke the bus pulled off the main highway once again. Sy made her way to the front of the bus to inquire about what had happened. She returned a moment later. "Looks like engine trouble. We'll be here a bit until they can get someone out to fix it."

The bandmates exited the bus, which was parked on the shoulder of the roadway. Cars and trucks whizzed by as they stood waiting for help to arrive. Flanking the freeway were endless rows of rice paddies, with carefully planted rows immersed in shallow water, separated every fifty feet by an elevated path. The paddies sat a few feet below the height of the road and were covered in a gentle mist.

As they stood by the road, Steve squinted and pointed toward the rice paddies. "Does that milk tea cause hallucinations?"

Allison followed his gaze. "I don't think so. What do you see?"

"I think I see more vending machines."

Allison squinted. As she did, a breeze kicked up and the mist parted. Sitting on an island in the sea of shallow water she could see a wooden shelter housing several vending machines. "I don't think you're hallucinating."

"My God. They're everywhere. I think they might be following us." He looked at the bottle of milk tea in his hand. "Yet somehow I'm okay with that." He began to make his way along one of the paths toward the vending machines. Allison followed, still somewhat uncertain whether the machines were real.

Steve and Allison returned to the bus with several bottles of milk tea. Rod and Ian were going back and forth about exactly how well-rehearsed Ian should be when he approached each of the girls.

"Well, I don't think I'd talk to them all at once, but if you want to, well, that's your call," Rod said definitively.

"I'm not certain I want to; I'm just asking if I should. I mean what if some of them are disappointed? What if I anger one of them but not the others? The repercussions are daunting. Absolutely daunting," Ian replied.

"I think this is a conversation you have one at a time," Allison added. "I mean, it's pretty personal."

"Yeah, but if I have a conversation with one, she'll tell the others. And then where are we?"

As Ian spoke a second bus pulled up behind the broken-down bus they had been on. Sy poked her head out of a window. "Okay. Ride's here. Let's go."

The band piled onto the new bus, which immediately pulled out into traffic. For the next couple hours, the band members slept. Allison, who had been sitting next to Rod, walked up the aisle and sat next to Ian. She nudged him awake. "I really think you need to talk to them as a group," she said as seriously as she could.

"That's bloody frightening. I'm just very worried about their response."

"Well, I don't see an alternative. If you tell them one at a time you've got a twenty-five percent chance you're talking to your daughter and a seventy-five percent chance you're not. You do it all at once, get it out in the open and clear the air."

Ian sighed and took off his glasses. He polished the lenses with the edge of his shirt. "Very well. It has to be done. I'll set them down and have a talk."

"One other thing. I think I should be there," Allison added.

———

Three more hours and two vending machines later, Uncle Joe's Band arrived in Fukuoka. They were greeted in the hotel lobby by Stygian Teal.

"How was the ride?" Sara asked Allison.

"Pretty boring. Except there were vending machines following Steve the whole way," Allison replied.

"Which I was perfectly okay with," Steve said. "I have discovered the ancient Japanese concoction designed to elevate the spirit known as milk tea. You should definitely try some."

"What was the shinkansen like?" Allison asked.

"It was cool. We rode on the Hello Kitty train. You got foot baths in the section of the train we were on. We're going to take it everywhere Sy will let us. You should come next time."

"If Sy lets me," Allison said as she grimaced.

As Allison spoke Sy raised her hand. "Okay, everyone. There's a restaurant here in the hotel. Eat tonight whenever you can. There's a conference room on the third floor where we'll meet tomorrow at eight. The turnaround is fast. We have shows tomorrow and the day after."

After Sy finished, Ian stood and cleared his throat. "Uh, yeah, I'd like to have a meeting this evening with you four." He pointed at the members of Stygian Teal. "Perhaps we can meet in the restaurant in an hour or so. I'll find a table."

After a brief uncomfortable silence Jane responded, "Sure. Can you tell us what for?"

Ian's brow furrowed. "Uh, no. I can't."

Jane looked at the other Stygian Teal members. "Okay. I guess we'll see you in an hour."

Ian nodded at Allison, who nodded back.

The restaurant in the Marquis Hotel in downtown Fukuoka was a staid and quiet place. Set with small tables, few dined there after midday. Hotel guests who had checked out earlier in the day had long since left, and those who checked in generally planned to eat elsewhere. Thus, when Ian arrived searching for a table in a secluded part of the establishment, it wasn't difficult to find one.

He arrived nearly a half hour prior to Stygian Teal, settled himself in the middle of the table, ordered some tea, and waited.

As Jane, Sara, Kara, and Indira made their way to Ian's table he stood. He pointed to the four seats placed across the table from him. "Ah yes, ladies, please sit so we can talk."

Stygian Teal sat slowly.

"Are we being kicked off the tour?" Sara asked.

Ian let out an anxious breath. "Heavens no. You've done great. You're part of the act. No, this has nothing to do with that. This is a bit more, um, personal."

As he spoke Allison arrived. Ian stood and pointed at a chair for her. "I've asked Allison to be her, for uh, context." Stygian Teal looked less concerned, but even more confused than when they had arrived.

After sitting, Ian spread out his hands on the table. He opened his mouth, but words didn't come out. As he started to utter a few discoordinated syllables the waitress arrived. "Um, would anyone like some tea?" he asked.

"Sure, yes, that would be great," Indira responded, before turning back to Ian. "Okay. We've got tea. Now what's going on?"

"You see, there was a time in my youth, in the early part of my career, where I lived a bit of what you might call a bohemian lifestyle." Ian stopped to see if his audience understood. When it was clear they hadn't, he continued. "I lived a life that was less, uh, respectable. I spent lots of time drinking and carousing."

Jane closed her eyes. "Yeah. You were a rockstar. So what?"

"Well, in the midst of that period of my life, I may have done some things that were, um, how shall I say? Rather irresponsible."

Ian looked again to see if his words were being understood.

Kara turned to Allison. "Allison, is he asking us to sleep with him? 'Cause we won't, it's offensive, and really it's gross."

Allison held up a hand. "No. It isn't anything like that. Just hear him out."

Ian cleared his throat. "In the course of my irresponsibility, I may have inadvertently slept with women who, through no one's fault, I didn't communicate with afterwards. Not that they did anything wrong, or that I was trying to be nefarious or anything like that. We just were briefly together and then we weren't."

Kara shrugged. "Yeah, so what? I've done that. We've all done that. Hookups are a thing. So what?"

Ian picked up his teacup and rolled it back and forth. "Yes, I suppose the difference is you didn't get pregnant."

The members of Stygian Teal looked at one another. Finally, Jane spoke. "So, you're a baby daddy. That's unfortunate, but you're not the first. When did you find out you have a kid?"

"It was right before we went on tour. Just a few short weeks ago."

Sara patted Ian's hand. "I'm sure it's been weighing on you. But understand you'll be a great dad and we don't judge you for the poor choices you've made."

Ian shook his head. "Bloody hell, that's not it. Listen, right before we went on tour, in fact the very night we met you all, I received a letter from this child's mother. She didn't sign it, so I'm not certain exactly who she was, but she noted some details, things only I would remember that make it hard to believe she was making it up." He paused, took a deep breath, and put the fingers of his hands together before continuing. "This child, a daughter, would be in her very early twenties and, according to the letter, is a member of Stygian Teal."

For a few moments there wasn't a sound. Kara, Sara, Indira, and Jane looked at Ian with blank faces.

"Are you saying you might be a father? To one of us?" Indira asked.

Ian nodded. "I'm afraid I might be."

Blank faces were punctuated by silence.

Suddenly Jane laughed. Her laugh started as a chuckle and gradually grew into a chortle and finally a full-throated belly laugh.

Then Sara began to laugh, then Kara and finally Indira. Their laughter permeated the entire restaurant, which, though mostly empty, stared at the table with five young women and a tall, gangly, middle-aged man with long black hair wearing round sunglasses and a black leather jacket.

Then, without warning, Ian stood up from the table and walked away.

———————

Despite becoming one of Japan's most notable artists, Joji never spent much time dealing with those who had declared his artistic greatness. He rarely watched television, listened to the radio, or engaged with media of any kind. At one point he obtained a cell phone, but one that did nothing other than allow him to call his mother. Utterly oblivious to his notoriety he sometimes found there were occasions where he found himself having odd conversations about the poetry he had so diligently placed throughout his journeys.

One such conversation happened inside an onsen near Sapporo where Joji had stopped for an afternoon lounging about in the pools and leisure space. As he sat alone and somewhat asleep in the pool of warm water, a young man approached and sat next to him. The pool was small and the man had a digital notebook in his hand, which seemed out of place in a pool of water.

"How are you able to work on your device in the onsen?" Joji asked.

"It's waterproof. From Sanyo. New kind of notebook. Completely waterproof." The man took the notebook and put it under the water as if to prove his point.

"Oh, that is very impressive," Joji replied.

"Yes. It is the latest technology. Now I can sit in the pool and get my work done. I can read and write."

"What do you read and write?" Joji asked, not certain why anyone would want to sit in a relaxing onsen pool working.

"I write about contemporary Japanese art. I write a column for the *Tokyo Times*. I write book reviews, report on cultural events, and interview various artists."

"That sounds very exciting. Who are your favorite artists?" Joji said as he leaned back against the edge of the pool.

"I have many. Recently I interviewed the movie director Hayao Miyazaki. It was a great honor to meet with such an artistic giant."

"I don't know many movies. Which ones were his?"

The man with the waterproof digital notebook looked as though he'd just discovered his digital notebook wasn't waterproof. "I'm sure you've seen them. *Totoro* is probably his most famous."

Joji thought for a moment. "Is that the one with the flying cat?"

"It isn't really a cat. It's a manifestation of a child's imagination made real."

Joji nodded. "Oh. I thought it was a giant floating cat. But what you said makes more sense. And I liked that movie."

The man with the waterproof digital notebook sighed. "Yes. It was a good movie. And he is a very good director."

Joji splashed some water up onto his face. The man picked up his digital notebook and began to read. After a moment Joji pointed to the notebook and asked, "What are you reading now?"

The man offhandedly replied, "I'm preparing to write about a poet."

Joji leaned forward. "I like poetry. Which poet are you referring to? Is he or she a well-known poet? What kind of poems do they write?"

The man stopped reading. "I am going to write about the poet Jo. Sometimes known as Jo Ojisan. No one knows who he is, just that he writes great haiku. Perhaps the greatest haiku of our age."

Joji smiled. "I write poetry too. And I sign it Jo, like Jo Ojisan."

"That's very nice. But no one knows who Jo Ojisan is. If we did, I would be able to interview him and find out how he comes up with such creative, insightful poetry."

"Yes. That is a problem. You do not know who he is. Has anyone tried to find out?"

The man looked slightly irritated. "Yes, yes of course. Many people have tried to find out who he is. There have been investigations. But none have been successful."

Joji frowned. "Well, it is unfortunate you can't interview him. Do you have some of his poetry?"

The man looked at his digital notebook. He scrolled through it. "Here is one from Sapporo." He showed it to Joji, who looked surprised. "I have written a very similar poem," he exclaimed.

The man looked at the poem again. "Well, perhaps you heard this one at some point and simply copied part of it. Sometimes people do that unconsciously."

Joji nodded. "Yes. That must be it. I must have heard it before and it came to the front of my mind when I wrote my own poem."

"Yes. Great pieces of literature can stick in parts of our minds and rise to the surface when we are thinking about something else. The great Jo Ojisan has clearly stuck in your mind. When did you read his work?"

Joji thought for a moment. "I'm not sure when I've read his poetry. Maybe you can read me a few more lines and that will jog my memory."

The man with the waterproof digital tablet scrolled through a few more pages before he stopped. "Here is something. A poem about factory workers.

> *Autumn factory*
> *For a human, great heart builds*
> *Watching the spark plug*

"Jo Ojisan is clearly trying to describe that the factory is getting old and he is showing solidarity with the workers' bad working conditions. It is a poem about the human spirit even when the factory doesn't treat its workers well."

Joji's eyes opened wide. "That sounds very much like a poem I wrote. It's remarkable just how much Jo Ojisan has influenced my own poems. I had no idea." He thought for a moment and then added, "But I don't think the poem is about bad conditions in a factory. I think it's just about how much the workers find meaning in their jobs."

The man with the waterproof digital tablet gave a knowing smirk. "Well, I'm sure we all interpret great poetry differently."

"Yes, perhaps my understanding of the poetry isn't as sophisticated as yours. Forgive my ignorance."

The man nodded. "We all take away what we can from the great poets." With that he picked up his waterproof digital tablet and moved to a different pool. Joji was left wondering where he had heard these remarkable poems and why he couldn't remember.

The two shows in Fukuoka were largely uneventful. Nothing was mentioned about the relationship between Ian and Stygian Teal.

During group meetings he remained focused on tasks at hand. With the rest of his band he made no mention of what had happened, and in return no one asked him about it.

After the second show Ian sat alone in a corner of the dressing room. Rick, Rod, and Steve were leaving to make their way back to the hotel when Allison entered the dressing room. She handed Ian a bottle of water. "Great show."

Ian took the water, opened the bottle, and took a swig. "Bloody good. Felt like I was faking it out there, so I'm glad it went over okay."

"You do seem a bit out of sorts when you're not onstage."

"Bloody moribund, more like."

Allison sat down next to Ian. "It's about the other night, isn't it?"

Ian took another swig of water. "I didn't exactly anticipate their response, did I?"

"Nope, I'm not sure anyone did."

"I just didn't think they'd find it so damned hilarious that I might be a father."

Allison sighed. "So, what are you going to do now?"

Ian shrugged. "Give up, I suppose. Maybe the letter was a fabrication. It was all a hoax. Who knows, perhaps they sent it themselves. All I know is I can't pursue this any further. We brought them with us specifically to be able to figure out which one might be my daughter and that doesn't seem likely to happen."

"Do you really want to give up?"

"It's not even about finding out whether I have a daughter, or which one it is, anymore. It's realizing they don't know or care if I'm their father. Bloody hilarious. Me, a father." Ian sighed and stood up. "Why don't you go back to the hotel? I'm going for a walk."

Allison stood, patted Ian's shoulder, and quietly left.

CHAPTER 16

Frogs and Monsters

Gotta catch 'em all
The dragonfly has landed
In the Game's pocket

—Jo Ojisan

"You'll be visiting a school here in Kobe" was the only instruction given by Sy. The bands had gathered around a table in the back of the hotel restaurant to discuss the day's events. "It'll be fun" was the only other reference made by Sy regarding their activity for the day.

It was under such auspices that both Uncle Joe's Band and Stygian Teal found themselves sitting in a large music room in the school. Upon arrival they had been greeted by the headmaster, a genial fellow, at least based on what their translator seemed to be interpreting. He had guided them on a quick tour, replete with a stop in every classroom to interrupt the proceedings for a quick wave and hello. Nine grades with two or three classrooms each proved to be grueling enough, but when the bands were seated directly in front of a middle-grade orchestra, complete with the sounds of prepubescent, off-key melodies, played with a vigor that shocked the heavy metal band, the two bands began to feel as though Sy hadn't been intentionally vague when she said, "It'll be fun."

Regardless, they gritted their teeth and smiled through the performances, even at one point picking up a few spare instruments and joining in. After being assailed by the orchestra, the bands were ushered into the school's cafeteria, replete with linoleum floors, plastic chairs, and folding tables. The bands were told to sit as nearly the entire school was herded in behind them.

"This is the welcoming ceremony," the translator said, nodding as though it were obvious.

The headmaster stood in front of the room and signaled the school to be quiet. He began to speak. As he did the translator spoke in a subdued voice. "It is an honor to have this famous American rock and roll bands visit our school. America and Japanese culture have long intertwined themselves with one another. The rock and roll music from America has been imitated by many Japanese musicians and performers. Some of you in this school may wish to become musicians. Though we may not teach rock and roll, you may learn musical skills here that can be used to create rock and roll music."

Steve leaned close to Ian. "I think Japan has a pretty good music scene. I don't think they're copying anything."

Ian smirked. "Think there was a translation problem, mate."

As the headmaster finished speaking, he bowed and waved for the band teacher to come to the front of the room. The band teacher, a small woman with a round face and generous smile, waved as she stepped in front of the school. She bowed to the bands. "It is a great honor to have such a wonderful group of musicians enjoy our band class today. Our young students are excited about the possibility that they too might someday become great musicians. We may not teach rock music in our orchestra, but we find it exciting and interesting." She bowed to the bands. "Thank you for visiting our school."

After she finished, the band teacher introduced a Mr. Matori, the vice principal. Mr. Matori had a bald head and was short, stocky, and very imposing. He had a thin mustache and wore a short-sleeved shirt with a tie. The translator informed the bands that Mr. Matori oversaw discipline at the school.

"He looks scary," Sara whispered to Jane.

As Mr. Matori began to talk, the room grew silent. Shuffling of feet and whispers stopped.

"He says that even though he doesn't listen to rock and roll music he approves of students listening to it when they are at home or on school grounds."

Ian looked at Steve.

As Mr. Matori continued to speak, Ian noticed the students were all looking at something on the floor. He could see that Kara was watching the students as well and trying to see what they were all looking at.

Mr. Matori continued, his speech increasing in intensity as he spoke. "I would like to point out the importance, which I'm sure our guests fully appreciate, of an education in classical music. It is imperative, which I'm sure our guests are aware of, that the rambunctious behaviors encouraged by rock and roll music is a problem and should be controlled."

The spot on the floor the students were watching moved a few feet toward the front of the room. Ian stared at it for a few moments. As it moved again Ian could make out the outline of a small frog. A few of the students pointed. The teachers pretended to not notice it. After a few more moments it hopped directly in front of the bands, not far from Mr. Matori, who was clearly so engaged in his speech he didn't notice.

The bands and students held their collective breaths as the frog jumped a few feet from Mr. Matori's feet.

"And we all know that rock and roll music has been used to incite rebellion and inappropriate behaviors that disrupt society."

When the frog jumped a few inches from Mr. Matori's shoe the students collectively gasped. Sara took a deep breath and raised her hand. Mr. Matori continued talking. As he began to turn from facing one side of the room to the next, he picked up his foot. Before he could put it down Sara and Indira lept from their seats and charged toward him. A look of surprise came over the vice principal's face as the two young women tackled him, knocking him on his back. The students gasped, stood, and then clapped.

As the vice principal slowly pulled himself to his feet the band teacher jumped in front of him and picked up the frog. Red faced, the vice principal stood. The band teacher held up the frog, pointed at Mr. Matori's shoe, and shook her head. Indira and Kara stood, dusted themselves off, and patted Mr. Matori on the back. The translator immediately stood in front of him, bowed, and began to apologize.

Mayhem gradually ensued. Students laughed and pointed. The band teacher laughed and began carrying the frog toward the door. Mr. Matori clenched his fists and stormed out of the cafeteria.

"Wonder what he's on about?" Ian asked, watching him leave.

"Yeah. He looked pissed. I would have thought he'd be happy he didn't end up stepping on a frog," Steve replied.

"We should go," the translator said, pointing toward a side door in the auditorium.

———————

Joji enjoyed Tokyo. Though generally solitary, he liked the bustle of the crowds, the giant buildings, the neon signs, and the general sense that it was the center of the world.

In 1990 Joji was sitting on a park bench in Ueno Park watching people walk by when a young man fell to the ground in front of him. As the young man fell, something flew from his hand and landed in Joji's lap.

The young man quickly rose to his feet. He looked at the ground around him, wondering where the object he had been holding landed.

"Are you looking for this?" Joji held up the small plastic box with buttons and a video screen that had fallen in his lap.

"Yes. Thank you." The young man took the device from Joji and started to take a step. As he did, he winced and hobbled to the bench next to Joji. "I think I hurt my knee," he said.

"Is it okay?" Joji asked.

"It will be. I just need to rest it for a moment," the man replied. "My name is Satoshi."

Joji nodded. "My name is Joji. It's nice to meet you. I'm curious. What was that box that fell out of your hand?"

Satoshi held it up. "It's a game. A video game."

Joji's eyes grew wide. "I've only played video games in an arcade."

"This one you can hold in your hand. It's called a Game Boy." Satoshi handed it to Joji. "Try it. It's fun."

Joji held it in his hand for a moment. The video screen showed a small ball bouncing up and down. The buttons moved the ball back and forth on the screen and pushed it around and kept it from going off screen. After trying it for a few moments he handed it back to Satoshi. "This is neat. How many games does it play?"

"I have four games, but I think there could be more," Satoshi replied. "And two people can play at once." He reached in his backpack and pulled out another Game Boy and a cord. He handed Joji the second Game Boy and plugged the cord into both.

On Joji's screen a character appeared. A moment later a second character appeared. Joji started pushing the buttons on his Game Boy and one of the characters began to jump and punch. As it did so the other character began to do the same. Soon the two characters were engaged and moving back and forth.

Joji and Satoshi played on the Game Boys for nearly two hours, at which point Satoshi's battery ran out and they were limited to a single device. As they finished, a dragonfly landed on the cable that connected the two consoles. Both young men looked at it as it started to move along the cord.

"I used to collect insects when I was younger," Satoshi commented.

"I like insects too," Joji added.

Satoshi reached his finger out close to the dragonfly, which moved from the cord to his finger. "Wouldn't it be great if there were a game where you could collect insects?" he said as he lifted the dragonfly up to look at it more closely.

"It would be something," Joji said. "I always thought of insects as little monsters. Very scary if they were giant, but nice when they are small."

"Yes, like Megalon in the Godzilla movie. He was very scary. But a tiny Megalon would be fun to collect." Satoshi lifted his finger and the dragonfly flew away. "When I was younger, I would put my insects in different glass bottles. I'd put holes in the lids so they had fresh air but could not escape. Then, on occasion, I would let them go."

Joji nodded. "That sounds like fun."

"Sometimes I would let two insects out together in a small bowl and see if they would fight or be friends." Satoshi picked up his backpack. "Some of them were nice, some not so nice. I learned the characteristics of each insect and saw what it did when I put one with another. Each species has its own powers and its own personality."

"What do you mean?"

Satoshi pointed to the dragonfly that had flown away. "For instance, dragonflies are very beautiful, but do not interact with other insects. They are loners. Ants don't attack other insects unless they are in groups. Beetles won't attack other insects but will attack other beetles. A mantis will attack anything."

"I once had a water bug. I don't think he attacked anything," Joji replied.

Joji and Satoshi sat quietly for a moment thinking about insects.

"You should create a video game where players collect insects," Joji asked.

"I'm not sure anyone would play."

Joji thought for a moment. "What if the insects weren't insects?"

"What do you mean?"

"What if they were little monsters? Like a small version of Megalon."

Satoshi nodded. "Yes, that might be a way to make them more interesting for players. You could have lots of different kinds of insects, or monsters, and the players would try and collect them."

Joji scratched his head. "You should have a device the players can put the monsters in while they collect them. Like the jar you use to collect insects."

"Yes. In the game it could be something that pulls the monster into it. Like a glass ball." Satoshi stood, clearly excited by the prospect of a new game collecting monsters. "The glass balls could be opened or closed whenever the player wanted to see their monster."

Joji tilted his head back, looking up at the sky. He could see mosquitos buzzing around a tree overhead. "There's only one problem."

"What's that?"

"It's a game. How do you determine who has won?"

Satoshi sat back on the bench. "It can't just be the player who collects the most wins. That would be boring. There must be some interaction between the two players."

"Or between their monsters. What if you put the monsters together, like you did with your insects?" Joji asked.

"That would work. The little monsters could fight with each other on behalf of their owners. The players collect their monsters and then use them to do battle." Satoshi put his backpack down on the bench, pulled out a notebook, and began to write. "Each monster could have different powers. There could be monsters that shoot energy at their opponents. And other monsters could make the ground move, or make plants grow, or make it rain. They could have all kinds of different powers."

Joji looked at Satoshi's notebook, which was quickly being filled with drawings of different kinds of monsters. "Remember they are supposed to be little monsters."

Satoshi nodded. "Yes, little monsters you can carry with you."

"Carry in your pocket," Joji replied. "Pocket monsters. That's what you should call them. Pocket monsters."

A decade after Joji and Satoshi sat on their park bench, Joji returned to Tokyo. After driving through the busy streets, he parked his van and made his way through the bustling crowds. Down through the central part of the city he walked, then up through the markets. Finally, in the business district he stopped to rest. Across the street he noticed a large sign on a building. The sign depicted a series of anime creatures next to a boyish-looking character holding a small red and white ball. At the top of the sign were the Nintendo corporate logo and a new word in Japanese that Joji hadn't seen before. After a moment of staring at the new word he smiled. The Japanese lettering had been abbreviated, from symbols that originally meant "pocket monsters" to the new word, "Pokémon."

That night Joji returned to the sign. With his paintbrush and can of white paint he lettered along the side of the building. The next morning, executives entering the building stopped and read Joji's poem. Several nodded, realizing it had been signed by famous haiku master Jo, and considered the wisdom of the great master in suggesting the catch phrase for their upcoming marketing campaign.

Sy found the bands sitting at the hotel bar late in the evening. Their laughter stopped when she entered the room.

"I thought you said it would be fun," Sara said. "You didn't say one of us might end up tackling the vice principal."

"I didn't think that you would. I certainly didn't suggest it."

"Did you know we'd be listening to the band?" Steve asked.

"No, but I'm not surprised." Sy smiled. "And think about how much those kids benefitted from having you there."

"Well, a bit of warning would have been helpful," Ian suggested.

"It might have. I would note, however, that I got a call from the school this evening." Sy paused to see how the two bands might respond. "They noted that your presence was well received, and they hoped there weren't any problems getting back." She paused again. Hearing no response she added, "and the frogs were fine."

CHAPTER 17

The Poet and the Moon

The oak tree: not interested
in cherry blossoms.

—Matsuo Basho (the wandering poet),
translated by Robert Hass

Uncle Joe's Band and Stygian Teal were slated to perform their final shows at the Nippon Budokan, a large octagonal arena set in the heart of Tokyo. Best suited for sporting events, the arena was occasionally used for large international tours. With fifteen thousand seats, it was the largest arena that Uncle Joe's Band had ever played. Four shows over a week had been scheduled.

Arriving a day early, both bands had a practice session at the venue prior to the upcoming performance. Allison spent most of the day intermittently working with the crew and playing her guitar with Stygian Teal. It wasn't until late in the evening when she made her way to the hotel restaurant to try and get dinner. At a table in a corner of the restaurant she found Stygian Teal sitting together having what appeared to be a heated conversation. As she approached, the group quieted.

"What's up?" Allison asked as she pulled up a chair.

Indira sighed. "We're working on some new material."

"You know you never told us where you came up with the ideas for your last set of new songs," Allison noted, a bit annoyed.

"We'll show you, but you have to keep it a secret," Sara said quietly, as though someone might be listening to their conversation.

"Okay. What is it?" Allison leaned forward, across the table.

Indira pulled a book out from a shoulder pack she had sitting beside her. "We found this in the gift shop at one of the hotels. It's brilliant. You can get inspired by almost anything here."

Allison picked up the book, *The Translated Works of the Artist Known as Jo*. She began carefully paging through it.

Jane pointed at a picture on one of the pages. "We were going to try and use this at some point but haven't really figured out how." The photo was of a series of Japanese characters painted on the side of a building. A caption underneath described the poem, a haiku, along with some commentary about how the Artist Known as Jo had managed to write such an illustrative piece of work, how the expert use of certain kanjis enhanced the meaning of the poem, several interpretations, and other details about the poem.

Allison read a few of the haikus out loud. She handed the book back to Jane. "Whoever this guy s, his writing is really profound."

Sara nodded. "We like the one about mourning the father in winter." Kind of dark and maybe a bit anti-patriarchal."

Allison sat back in her chair. "Yeah. I wanted to talk to you all about that. Specifically, about the conversation you had with Ian."

Indira took a drink of tea. "You mean about the dad thing?"

"Yes."

The table was quiet for a moment.

Jane cleared her throat. "Look, Allison, I understand there may be a lot of meaning in finding out who your dad is, for you, but I don't really have that issue. I haven't known who my father is since I was born and, frankly at this point I really don't care to know. My mom raised me alone. She had the occasional boyfriend and some of them stuck around long enough I got to know them, but otherwise I really don't care. If he didn't worry about me, I wouldn't really feel too worried about him."

Kara nodded. "Yup. That's one thing we all have in common. We were raised by strong women and didn't really see the need for a father."

Allison sighed. "Yeah, that's how I felt. Until I met my dad."

Jane crossed her arms. "I know you've got a good relationship with him, but aren't you a bit angry he wasn't around?"

"That's complicated. My mom wasn't exactly a model parent. I was mostly raised by my grandparents. She never told me about my dad, even when I asked. And it turns out she knew who he was; she just didn't care enough to tell me."

"So how did you find out about Rod?" Sara asked.

"One summer I was supposed to go stay with my mom and she dropped me off and told me I'd be staying with my dad instead. I wasn't even sure who he was when she dropped me off."

"You mean she dropped you off with the band and you weren't even sure which one was your dad?" Indira asked with a surprised look on her face.

"Yup. That's how it started. Wasn't until after I got home that I figured out which one was my dad. I had to get my birth certificate. It listed my father as 'a guitarist', I even confronted my mother about it, but she just said she didn't remember."

Allison stopped talking for a moment and the table grew silent once again. Kara picked up the small teapot in the middle of the table and poured herself more tea. Sara rubbed a pair of chopsticks together. Jane looked down at her hands.

Finally, Indira spoke. "Are you sure he's your dad?"

Allison smiled. "Yes. To be certain we took a paternity test. When it came back, I made my mom add him to the birth certificate."

Jane shook her head. "Wow. That's crazy."

Once again, the table was silent. Allison took a teacup from an adjacent table and poured herself some tea. She cleared her throat. "Look, I'm not telling any of you what to do, but I know Ian was really embarrassed when he brought up the letter. When you all laughed, he got pretty upset."

Jane nodded. "I didn't mean to upset him, I just didn't know what to say, so I just laughed."

"I think that's what we all did," Sara added.

Allison took another drink of tea. "Well, I think it's fine if you don't want to reveal which one of you is his daughter, assuming you know, but just realize it's a sensitive topic."

"For whatever it's worth, I know he isn't my father," Sara said. "My mom has made it pretty clear my dad lives in Colorado." She paused. "I'll tell Ian."

Jane crossed her arms. "One thing bothers me about all this. Did they invite us on the tour just to find out which of us is Ian's daughter?"

Allison shook her head. "No, Sy would never allow that. They did come to see you that first night to find out, but they assumed there would only be one girl in the band."

The Stygian Teal bandmates laughed.

Allison continued, "But they really thought you guys were good. And the punk sound fit well as an opening act."

"That makes me feel better," Sara said.

"One other question. Can we see the letter?" Jane asked.

During most of his adulthood, Joji didn't seek meaning in any given place. The sites he visited, the cities, forests, rivers, and villages, just simply happened to be there when he passed through. Place and movement weren't an object of Joji's lifestyle so much as a search for something. Something he could never quite identify, nor even describe. Some might have said he searched for himself, others for purpose. A few might say he was looking for meaning. While these descriptions might capture some element of his search, they weren't accurate. For many years, Joji himself didn't know. He simply wandered.

One day outside of Kyoto his search gained clarity. He had parked his van near a forest on a hillside and, for reasons unknown to him, began to climb into the wooded hills. He passed a small creek and a house with an elderly couple planting flowers outside their small house. He stumbled up a gravel path into a small clearing.

In the middle of the clearing was a tiny house, covered nearly completely in moss, with a rotting waterwheel on one side and a stone chimney at its side. Behind the house sat a small well, with a rope and bucket. Joji sat on a stone near the well.

Without warning an old man sat on a rock next to Joji. He was wearing a tattered traditional robe; held a walking stick in his left hand and a leaf in his right. He smiled at Joji, a toothless, warm smile.

Joji bowed his head. "Hello, I am Joji."

The old man bowed in response "Welcome to my home."

"It is a very nice home. Very secluded, here in the forest."

The old man continued to smile. "I have only stayed here a single night. But it is a nice home."

Joji tilted his head. "You've only stayed in your home one night?"

The old man nodded.

"That seems like a very short time to live in a house."

"I liked to travel."

Joji nodded. "So do I. Where did you go?"

"Everywhere, I think. I followed the moon."

Joji thought for a moment. "The moon is very beautiful. I too have looked in many places to see the moon at night."

The old man continued to smile. Joji noticed for a moment how pale his hands appeared. As he looked up Joji noticed words had been carved into a rock near the house. He pointed to them. "There are words written on that rock. I can't read them from here. What do they say?"

"It says, 'Stillness. The cicada's cry. Drills into the rocks."

Joji sat up. "Oh, you are a poet."

The old man looked thoughtful for a moment. "Some would say I am. Though I think I am simply a man looking for the moon."

Joji stood and bowed. "I am a poet as well. It is an honor to meet you."

"You are a poet. Where do you write your poems?" the old man asked.

"I mostly paint them. With a brush and some white paint. I paint them on things: buildings, trees, pieces of wood, whatever I can find."

"Do you like to paint?"

"Not really, but I think the letters look alive when they are painted." Joji thought for a moment. "I mean when they are painted in white."

"Like rays of light from the moon."

"Yes, like rays of light from the moon." Joji turned and looked at the old man. He noticed his deep dark eyes. Eyes that penetrated so deep Joji thought he could feel them examining his soul. Yet despite their intensity, the old man's eyes were kind, as though he somehow saw beauty and goodness in things, even in those places where others didn't.

"Why did you become a poet?" Joji asked.

"Why does the wind blow? Why does the fish swim? I am a poet because that is what I was created to be."

Joji nodded. "And why do you travel so much? Are you looking for things to write about?"

"No. Like I said, I am looking for the moon. The moon is my

muse and I write whenever it tells me to. Sometimes it's at night; sometimes it's the day."

"I write about whatever happens to me," Joji replied. "Sometimes things happen that are good; sometimes they are bad. But I often feel the need to write them down."

"This is the way of things. You were created to perceive the world, and then reveal your perceptions. Like water in the brook, you cannot move without telling others. For people like us, it is our way."

Joji looked at his hands. "I think others see me as strange, or different. As though I'm not supposed to be this way. My parents, my friends, everyone I know thinks I should settle down and get a job."

"You cannot." The old man turned back to look at the house. "There are many trees in the forest. Pear trees make pears that are good to eat. Cherry trees grow beautiful blossoms that scatter like snow in the late spring. The pine makes needles to soften the ground. And the oak grows gnarled and strong. The oak cares not for pears, or cherry blossoms or soft ground. It grows in its own way, in its own time." The old man turned his gaze back to Joji. "This is why you cannot change. You are the oak and must grow in your own way, in your own time. Only then will you find that which you seek."

"Have you found what you have been looking for?"

The old man closed his eyes. "I have."

"How? How did you find it?" Joji tilted his head. "And how did you know when you'd found it?"

The old man looked at his house. "There was a point where I simply stopped looking. It was at that moment that it became clear: I didn't need to find the best place to see the moon; I simply needed to wait, and the moon would find me. When you look for something, sometimes it is best to wait and it will come to you."

The old man looked back at Joji. "What do you seek?"

Joji shrugged. "I don't know."

The old man smiled. "Then wait for it. It will find you. Why do you write poems?"

Joji thought for a moment. "I'm not sure, really. I just feel something inside me that needs to come out. I have something I need to say, and if I don't put it into words and say it to the entire world, I won't be able to live with myself."

The old man nodded. "You must say those things in your heart.

You cannot let them stay and fester." He looked directly at Joji. "Never stop what you are doing. Never stop being who you are or saying what you say. Yours will be a beautiful life, as long as you are willing to let it." With that he stood, picked up his walking stick, and slowly ambled toward the dilapidated house.

"I didn't catch your name," Joji called after him.

The old man looked over his shoulder. "Matsuo. Matsuo Basho."

As Joji watched, the old man slowly dissipated into the moss and the ferns and the rocks surrounding the cabin.

CHAPTER 18

Costume Act

Face paint makeup layered on
My persona gettin' along
Lookin' like I don't' belong

—Stygian Teal, "Masks"

The first performance in Nippon Budokan took place with the usual fanfare and excitement that surrounded most of Uncle Joe's Band's performances. Stygian Teal led off the show with one of their new songs followed by the series of songs that made up their standard playlist. The young crowd was mostly well behaved, but by the end of the show a mosh pit of sorts had developed in front of the stage.

At first the Bodukkan's security guards tried to prevent the young people from slamming their bodies against each other, but it wasn't long before they gave up and simply patrolled the perimeter of the dancing hoard, trying to ensure order everywhere else.

When Stygian Teal finished and left the stage, Allison and the crew began the process of tearing down equipment and preparing for Uncle Joe's Band. When she was done, she made her way to the dressing rooms backstage and knocked on the band's door. It opened and Rod, Rick, and Steve each gave her a hug as they exited and headed toward the stage. After a moment of waiting for Ian to emerge, Allison entered the room to find him sitting, looking at himself in the mirror.

"It's time to go on," Allison said.

"Right," Ian responded. He continued to stare into the mirror. "I'm not really feeling it tonight."

"Well, that crowd is, so you'd better get yourself together and get out there."

Ian sighed and sank back into one of the folding chairs that were scattered around the room. "And what if I don't, 'eh? What if I decide I've had enough and I don't want to sing anymore? Maybe I just sit in 'ere and let everyone else have their bit of fun without me."

Allison folded her arms. "Look, you're a little off. A bit upset perhaps. Not yourself. Unfortunately, you've chosen to be a great rock and roll artist, which means there are lots of people who've paid their hard-earned money to come see you perform. And I don't think even in your current state that deep down you want to let them down. Right?"

Ian shrugged. "I don't know, love. I'm just not feeling it tonight."

Allison sighed and rolled her eyes. "Okay, look, they want to see the letter."

Ian took off his sunglasses. "What?"

"They want to see the letter. They want to look at the letter. From their mother."

Ian stood up. "Really. Wow. Well, what else did they say?"

Allison's mouth curled up in a smile. "It's not Sara. She knows her father."

Ian nodded. "Not Sara. That leaves Kara, Indira, and Jane." He put his sunglasses back on. "And they want to see the letter."

Allison pointed toward the door. "Yes. They want to see the letter. And the audience wants to see you. So why don't you get out there and scream some lyrics at them."

Ian nodded. "Yes. I should scream some lyrics at them." He reached inside his leather jacket and pulled out an envelope. "And they want the letter." He handed the envelope to Allison. "You'll give it to them, right?"

After the show Allison found Stygian Teal in their dressing room sipping water and talking about how the new songs had been received. Allison didn't say a word, but simply entered the room, placed the envelope with the letter on the table, and left.

Two hours later Allison's phone began to buzz. She initially ignored it, but after the third series of rings she picked it up. She could hear Ian's muffled voice on the other end.

"So, what did they say?" he asked, as if it was a clandestine question.

"They didn't say anything. I just gave them the letter and left."

Ian was quiet for a moment. "Nothing. They didn't say a bloody thing?"

"Like I said, I just gave them the letter and left. They didn't say a thing."

"What the bollocks do we do now? I would have thought they would have said something."

Allison rolled her eyes. "Now we wait. We don't do anything. We just wait. They need to absorb what they see."

"I think we should try wearing stage makeup with some outlandish costumes," Jane said as she pulled the green and blue hat off the rack.

"Costumes and crazy stage makeup are a terrible idea," Rod replied.

"Yes, truly terrible," Steve added.

"Well, what about KISS and that whole era of glam rock?" Sara asked.

Ian folded his arms. "For starters, KISS was amazing because they could pull it off. There were a whole series of bands that tried, and ultimately failed. The KISS guys were the only ones. And musically, well how should I put this, the fact that a band uses gimmicks like makeup or costumes just reveals a certain musical inadequacy."

Jane cleared her throat. "Like David Bowie?"

Steve looked at Rod. "Yes, there are exceptions. But for the many who have tried, few have succeeded."

Rod put his hand on Jane's shoulder. "You have to trust us on this one. We've gone down that road. It didn't end well. For anyone."

Indira tilted her head. "Why, what did you guys do?"

Ian took off his sunglasses and began cleaning the lenses. "Well, you see, we went through a phase, you know, a period where we were experimenting. Sort of a 'throw it to the wind and see if it comes back' kind of period."

"And like pissing into the wind, it did come back," Rick added.

Sara shot Jane a we-have-to-find-out-about-this look. "What did you decide to wear?"

Rick shook his head. "It's not so much what we decided to wear, but who else thinks it's a good idea to wear it."

Ian nodded. "Yes. That's the thing. You must make certain you're wearing the appropriate items in the right place. It's when you wear the wrong things in the wrong place, things that go awry."

Rod sighed. "We went to perform in Berkeley and we figured, 'Well, this is a very left-wing place. Let's have some kind of costume that protests something.' There was a big effort to clean up the oceans at the time so we thought we'd try a nautical theme."

Rick shook his head. "Not so much nautical as 'ocean garbage.'"

Rod grimaced. "Well, yes, ocean garbage. Anyway, we went to the port in Oakland where they dump all the junk that gets snagged on ships after they've crossed the Pacific. Buoys, fishing nets, floating pieces of debris, pretty much anything you could think of that might be in an ocean landfill."

Steve coughed. "Then we simply attached some of the best bits to some old clothes."

"So, you attached garbage from the beach onto your clothes to make some kind of statement?" Sara asked.

"Exactly. It was supposed to be a statement. Kind of a 'hey look at all the junk humans dump in the ocean,'" Rod said as he shook his head. "When we got to the show, we looked like a bunch of fishermen who'd gotten tangled up in their lines."

Rick sighed. "There was a dead fish stuck on Ian. I think it was rotten. Stunk terribly."

Sara's brow furrowed. "I think there's a difference between the costumes KISS wore and an awkwardly attempted political statement."

Indira nodded. "Yeah, I mean you guys are a metal band. Why would you think something like that was a good idea?"

Rick closed his eyes. "It seemed like a good idea at the time."

Steve rolled his eyes. "That was nothing compared to the gig at the Barren Tortoise."

"We don't talk about the Barren Tortoise," Rod added.

Indira looked at Jane. "I really want to know about the Barren Tortoise."

Ian looked sideways at Steve. "We do not discuss the Barren Tortoise."

Steve shook his head. "We wore the wrong colors to the wrong bar."

Ian touched his left shoulder. "Got me blimey shoulder dislocated from that one."

Steve continued. "We thought we'd wear a bunch of silver and black KISS-like makeup to the Barren Tortoise in 2000. It was a December evening as I recall. Rick and Ian had these weird jackets with spikes all over them."

"Great jackets, they were." Ian added.

"So, what went wrong? That sounds better than wearing fishnets, with actual fish in them."

Steve looked at Jane. "Do you know where the Barren Tortoise is?"

Jane looked at Indira. "I think it's near Hunter's Point?"

Steve nodded. "That's right. And what else is in Hunter's Point?"

Jane sucked in a breath and put her hand over her mouth to hide a smile. "Holy crap!"

"What?" Indira shook her head.

"The old Candlestick Park is near Hunter's Point. It's where the 49er's used to play before they moved to Santa Clara." Jane started to laugh. "They wore black and silver to a 49er's bar."

Steve closed his eyes. "Not only was it a 49er's bar, but the Raiders had beaten the 49er's a couple nights before. We walked in, looking like outsized Raiders fans, among a bar full of angry 49er's supporters."

Ian touched his shoulder again. "They thought we were there to point and laugh. We didn't even make it ten paces inside the bar before a melee started."

Rod grimaced. "When we left every bit of silver and black had been removed and someone had dumped red and gold glitter on Ian's head."

Ian scratched his head. "Sometimes I still have some glitter falling out."

Rod didn't think he'd ever heard Sy sound panicked. Usually, unflappable even in the most trying circumstance, she never gave a hint of whatever underlying emotion was brewing beneath her calm demeanor. But today she genuinely sounded frightened and flustered when she told Rod the bands needed to have an emergency meeting immediately.

Uncle Joe's Band walked into the hotel lobby to find Sara, Indira, Kara, Sy, and Allison huddled together whispering with quiet intensity. Rod cleared his throat and the whispering stopped.

"What the devil's going on?" Ian asked. "And where is Jane?"

Sy and Allison exchanged glances. Allison looked directly at Ian. "Jane's gone. We don't know where she went."

Steve pointed at Sy. "What do you mean she's gone? Where did she go?"

Allison continued. "She and Kara were sharing a room. When Kara got up this morning Jane had left and taken all her stuff with her. We've all tried calling her but she won't pick up." She pointed at the other members of Stygian Teal and Sy.

"Do you think she decided to go home?" Ian asked.

"We don't know."

Rod looked at Kara. Her arms were folded and she looked like she was going to cry. "What did you talk about last night?"

"We talked about your letter."

Indira looked up. "Yeah. Now that I think about it, she was really quiet when we were discussing it."

Sara nodded. "The three of us were all certain you weren't our father. She kind of went along with that, nodded a bunch like she felt the same way, but didn't say much."

"And that isn't very Jane-like," Indira added.

Sy took a deep breath and closed her eyes. "I'm not really sure what to do here. Do we just not do the opening act? If not, we're breaking our agreements with the record company. Do we try to find her? If we do find her, are we supposed to convince her to come back?"

"We find her," Ian replied.

Rod nodded, then sighed. "Where do we look?"

Allison flopped down in a chair. "There has to be somewhere in Tokyo where she'd go." She pulled out her phone and began tapping on the screen. "I know there's someplace here that she'd go. A place that would give her peace."

Indira shook her head. "She wasn't a big fan of anything in Tokyo."

The room grew quiet. Suddenly Allison stood up. She handed her phone to Ian and pointed at the screen. "She's here."

Ian took off his sunglasses and stared for a moment. "Here? What's bloody here?"

The others huddled around, peering over Ian's shoulders.

"Yeah, what the heck is that? And why would she go there?" Kara wondered aloud.

Allison's eyes narrowed. "Totoro."

CHAPTER 19

Neko

Fifty ways to skin a cat
Nine lives now and more after that

—Uncle Joe's Band, "Got Your Tongue"

At some point in the mid-1990s Joji found a companion. In the middle of a cold winter's night somewhere west of Kobe, he was awakened by a scratching sound on the door of his van. Not seeing anyone there, he rolled over and started to go back to sleep when he heard it again. Seeing no one, he opened the door. As he did a scrawny Calico leaped into the front seat and began to lick its paws.

Joji found a towel and began to dry the animal off when it started to purr. With little hesitation it climbed into the back of the van, curled up and went to sleep. The next morning it remained in the same spot and only rose when it could smell Joji eating some chicken and rice. Not wanting to be perceived as an impolite host, Joji set the cat next to the van and placed a can with some chicken in front of it. As the cat began to eat, Joji climbed in the van, started the engine, and began to drive away. For several minutes he drove, certain the cat had been left far behind.

As he rounded a corner he glanced at the passenger's seat and was shocked to see the Calico grooming itself. He tried to put the cat outside the van again. After setting it on the side of the road, he climbed back in the van and as he prepared to leave, he heard a rustle behind his seat. Turning around he saw the cat as it hopped from the back seat to the front.

For the next couple of years, the cat rode alongside Joji from one end of Japan to the other, usually curled up on the passenger seat, waking only to step outside at the beginning or end of the day. Whatever Joji ate, the cat ate. Wherever Joji slept, the cat slept. It followed him when he left the van and led him back as he returned.

Joji never considered giving the cat a name. He often wondered what its name was, or if it was a stray that simply hadn't been named by a human owner, or whether the cat had conceived a name for itself in its own mind and simply couldn't tell anyone. Whatever the case, Joji didn't think it was appropriate to simply come up with a name that the cat might not appreciate, so he reverted to simply calling the cat "Neko" ("Cat" in Japanese).

The cat was an omnipresent part of Joji's life.

Until the day he met Hayao.

————————

Joji had decided to spend the end of summer in Tokyo. As the days shortened and nights grew cooler, he liked parking his van next to various parks and other greenspaces where he could lay about in the sun during the day watching Neko chase birds and small rodents.

One lazy afternoon Joji and Neko sat on the grass at Inokashira Park when a large kite dropped from the sky and landed in front of them. It was orange and yellow, shaped like an airplane. As they watched, a middle-aged man with a beard ran toward them spooling the twine the kite was attached to.

"My apologies for landing my kite so close to you," the man with the beard said as he approached Joji.

"No problem," Joji replied. As if prompted by the man's concern, Neko jumped on the kite and began playing with the string the man had continued to spool. Joji picked Neko up and took the string from him.

"Your cat likes the string," the man noted.

Joji nodded. "Yes. He seems to like the string and your kite. I'm sorry if he's broken it."

"No problem. What is a kite if not a plaything?"

The man picked up the kite. "My name is Hayao. What is yours?"

"I'm Joji."

"And what is the name of your cat?"

Joji looked at Neko. "He doesn't really have a name. I just call him Neko."

Hayao smiled. "Neko is a fine name. Very descriptive."

Joji set Neko on the ground. The calico immediately began rubbing Hayao's leg. Hayao reached down and began to pet him. Neko purred.

"I am looking for a cat," Hayao said.

"Neko is a good pet," Joji replied

"I'm not necessarily looking for a pet. I need a cat model," Hayao added.

Joji tilted his head to one side. "A model?"

"Yes. I am making a movie with a cat spirit in it. It is an animated movie and I need a live cat on which I can model the character."

Joji looked at Neko. "Do you think he looks like a spirit?"

Hayao smiled. "He looks like a cat."

"What does the spirit cat do?" Joji asked.

"The story is about children who get lost and meet spirits in the forest. A cat spirit helps them find their way back to their parents. It's about children's imagination, fears, and hope."

Hayao set the kite on the ground next to Neko. The cat continued to purr and jumped back on the kite.

"That sounds like a nice story."

"Yes. I think I'm going to have one of the spirits fly like a kite. When the children need to find their parents, they get on the kite and fly to see them."

Joji reached down to pet Neko. "Perhaps the kite could look like a cat?"

Hayao nodded. "That is an excellent idea. I thought the kite might look like a plane, but perhaps it might look like the cat spirit."

Neko jumped off the kite and began rubbing Hayao's leg again. He reached down and began to pet him.

Joji folded his arms. "Why would the cat spirit look like a kite? Or for that matter a plane? After all, it's a spirit. It doesn't need wings to fly?"

"I wanted the children to fly in something they would like. Something they wouldn't be afraid of," Hayao replied.

Joji looked around the park. People walked along trails, sat together on the grass, and paddled about on small boats. On one of the playgrounds groups of children played. Several wore school uniforms. As he watched, a woman in a blue sweater, presumably a teacher, began to herd the uniformed children together and shepherd them toward a white bus parked near the playground. The children danced and skipped toward the bus. When the bus door opened, they crowded their way onto the bus, smiling and laughing.

"The cat spirit should be a bus," Joji said.

"A bus?" Hayao asked.

"Yes. Children like to ride on buses. The cat spirit could turn into a bus for the children to ride on. It could be furry, like the cat. And fly. The cat spirit bus should fly."

Hayao closed his eyes and scratched his chin. After a moment he murmured, "Yes, I can see that. The cat spirit turns into a flying bus that the children climb aboard." He opened his eyes and turned to Joji. "This is a very good suggestion."

Neko stopped rubbing Hayao's leg and flopped down on the ground.

Hayao bent down to rub Neko's back. "I like your cat. Would he be willing to spend time with me? As a model?"

"That's up to him," Joji replied.

"What do you mean? He's your cat."

"Neko is his own cat. He follows me when he wants to and will follow someone else when he is ready."

Hayao picked up his kite. "Well, let's see what he does." He began to walk away.

For a moment Neko hesitated, looking at Joji, before turning and following Hayao.

Joji sat in the park for another hour before returning to his van and driving away, alone.

Ian walked slowly down Kichijoji Avenue. The tall green trees of Inokashira Park rocked back and forth with the wind as he stopped and gazed across a grassy slope. At the bottom of the slope a wandering pond was filled with small, swan-shaped paddle-boats that slowly splashed their way from one side to the next.

Ian made his way into the park, wandering along a path next to the pond, moving back and forth, peering at each of the boats, trying to see Jane. He wandered through a forest of cherry trees beginning to blossom.

Passersby strolling on the same path as Ian stopped and stared at his lithe, six-foot frame wearing a black leather jacket, black jeans, and black sunglasses. Set against the idyllic park they might have wondered if he were an angel of death, sent to find the unfortunate soul who wouldn't survive their midafternoon sojourn.

Along the park's path Ian wandered, looking left and right for any sign of Jane. He passed a playground and a food stand. In a small clearing a bronze sign pointed toward a gate. Ian entered the gate and stepped into a small courtyard surrounded by buildings of different architectural designs. A building with stucco cottage-like doors and windows was opposed by a futuristic glass and steel structure that might have been well placed in Tokyo's financial district. In the middle of the courtyard stood a ticket booth with a large glass window framing a person-sized black and orange cartoon cat.

Ian stopped at the ticket booth, but seeing no response from the cat, he walked past it, through a large door and into a foyer with a vaulted ceiling and several large statues of cartoon characters. A series of kanjis were on a large sign which in smaller font read "The Ghibisi Museum."

Slowly Ian made his way through various rooms, each themed with a different group of characters and the title of a movie. Ian was quite certain he hadn't seen any of them. The museum was mostly empty, with the occasional gaggle of grade-school children huddled around some exhibit or another.

Ian entered the room on the third floor of the futuristic building to find a giant furry Totoro cat shaped like a bus. As large as a king-sized bed, the cat-bus sat next to a wall-sized picture of the same cat-bus in the movie.

In a corner of the cat-bus Ian could see a body curled in the fetal position. "Jane?"

The body moved a bit.

Ian pulled himself up onto the flat surface of the bus. It was softer than he expected and he sunk deeply into the soft fur. He tried to pull himself up further but couldn't manage. He cleared his throat. "Uh, Jane?" As he pulled himself back, he rocked up to try and free himself from the deep cushion hole into which he had fallen. "Jane. I think I'm stuck." The body rolled on its side and Jane's head appeared.

"Ironic, don't you think?" she asked.

"That I'm stuck in a giant couch that looks like a cat."

"It's not a couch. It's Totoro."

Ian tried once again to sit up. After a brief struggle he collapsed back into his cat-bus cushion hole. "Right then. I'm stuck in Totoro. I'm not sure what a Totoro is, but apparently, I can't get out of it."

As Ian spoke a group of uniformed schoolchildren entered the room. Upon seeing the giant cat-, gasps and cries of joy rang out. A few of the children leaped up on the cat-bus and began jumping on it; the remainder stood in a semi-circle around Ian, eyes wide wondering whether the mystical ghost cat had brought a somewhat darker part of the spirit world back with him.

After the children grew tired of jumping on the Totoro cat-bus they began to climb off and move to the next room. As they did Ian rolled onto his side and began pushing himself off the front of Totoro's flat, cushioned sitting area. As he did his foot caught on an ear and he fell backward off the cat-bus and onto the floor.

As he lay on his side Ian saw Jane's head poke over the side. "Are you okay?" she asked.

Ian tried to pull himself up, but after a moment winced and sat back on the floor. "I think I hurt my back," he said, grimacing.

Jane pulled her legs over the edge and jumped to the floor next to Ian. "You know only children twelve and under are supposed to get on Totoro."

"Lovely. I broke my back on a giant fluffy children's toy."

Jane sighed. "I was really having a nice time."

"You were curled up in the fetal position."

Jane sat on Totoro's head. Her eyes began to well up with tears.

Ian, with some difficulty, pulled himself up on his elbows. "It's you, isn't it?"

Jane nodded and started to sniffle.

CHAPTER 20

Fathers and Daughters

Fevers high, fevers low
See the Doctor, that's where we'll go
Fevers high, fevers low
Need some meds, now we need some mo'

—Uncle Joe's Band, "Malpractice"

When the ambulance arrived at the Ghibli Museum the paramedics had some difficulty lifting Ian onto the stretcher. Every small motion was followed by a "bloody hell" and "bollocks" with the occasional expletive randomly added. As the paramedics rolled the stretcher past the museum's personnel, a rather stern woman looked at Jane, said something in Japanese, and pointed to the sign indicating that only children under the age of twelve were supposed to climb on Totoro. Jane shook her head and made an unkind gesture toward the woman, who rolled her eyes and walked away.

The ambulance ride was short and Ian was more relaxed by the time he was rolled into the Emergency Room. In contrast Jane appeared worried. As Ian was moved from the stretcher to a bed in a small room, she stood in the hallway asking anyone who looked like a nurse or an orderly for help. After being ignored for several minutes a man in a long white coat with a stethoscope hanging from his neck stepped past her and into the room with Ian.

"Good afternoon. I'm Doctor Hanashi. I understand you hurt your back."

Ian turned his head. "You speak English."

"I did my residency at Texas A and M."

"You're an Aggie?"

Doctor Hanashi nodded. "Aggie through and through."

Ian took off his sunglasses. "What residency did you do?"

"Obstetrics and gynecology."

Ian grimaced. "Obstetrics. I'm bloody sure I'm not pregnant."

"Yeah, but I'm the only physician who speaks English."

Ian tried to sit up. "Fine, just don't tell me to push."

Jane stepped in the room. "Can you fix him?"

Doctor Hanashi smiled. "Maybe." He motioned for Ian to try and sit up.

Ian pulled himself to the side of the bed and dropped his legs down. He slowly twisted himself around to be able to sit on the side of the bed. Doctor Hanashi touched his back in several places, had him lift his legs and turn around. He pressed his fingers into the small of Ian's back until Ian exhibited a howl.

"In my professional opinion you strained your back." He looked at Jane. "Or he might be in labor."

Jane looked puzzled.

Doctor Hanashi nodded toward Ian. "We'll check an x-ray We'll give him a muscle relaxant and let him sit for a bit."

After Doctor Hanashi left, a nurse walked into the room, helped Ian lay back onto the bed, and started an IV in his arm. A few moments later he was wheeled away for an x-ray. When he returned Jane wasn't in the room.

The nurse entered the room with a syringe.

"What happened to the girl who was just here?" Ian asked.

The nurse shook her head.

Ian pointed to the chair. "The girl who was there. Where is she?"

The nurse moved the chair closer to Ian's bed. He shook his head. "No, no. The girl in the chair. Where did she go?" he pointed toward the door. The nurse picked up the chair and moved it out of the room. Ian sighed and collapsed back in his bed, discouraged. The nurse reentered the room and inserted the syringe into the IV and pressed the plunger. After a few moments Ian visibly relaxed.

"Are you okay?" Jane asked.

"Actually, much better," Ian responded. He looked down at his toes. "I don't feel my feet."

Jane moved closer to the bed. "Why did you come looking for me?"

Ian opened and closed his eyes. "Yeah, about that. I was worried about you. You know, you left and we were worried and you know I just thought, well you know, maybe it had something to do with the letter. And me." He looked at Jane.

Jane looked away. "Yeah."

Ian sighed. "Look, I don't really know how to do this. Believe me, if I had known, things would be bloody different." He tried to sit up but fell back into bed.

"Did you know?"

"No. Until I saw the letter, I had no idea I even had a daughter. Even then I didn't believe it." He paused, held up his IV, and looked at it. "It's odd, but somehow when I first saw you sing I kind of knew. I'm not sure why. Not sure what it was, but somehow, I felt something. Some kind of connection."

"Why did you come looking for me?"

"Because you left and we have a show…"

Jane held up a hand and shook her head. "No. Why did you come looking for me when you got the letter? You hadn't ever seen me before, hadn't been there when I was growing up or when I was ten and started learning to sing or when my mom's boyfriend beat the crap out of her and I had to leave in the middle of the night or…" Her voice trailed off. She cleared her throat. "Why did you come looking for me?"

Ian was silent for a moment, surprised at the question. "I don't know. At first, I just didn't believe I might have a daughter. I wasn't sure, you see. But the possibility isn't something you can ignore. The idea that somewhere there might be a child, a young woman, who was at least a little like me, well, I had to go find out if it was real." He took a deep breath. "The strange thing is, when we first saw you play, I knew it was you."

"Where were you?"

Ian closed his eyes again, not certain whether the muscle relaxants were kicking in. "I was back at the hotel, getting ready."

"No. Where were you when I was growing up?"

Ian shook his head. "Obviously not where I should have been. I didn't know." He paused, noting that he was becoming a bit verklempt. "I'm not sure you would have wanted to know me when you were growing up. I was an awful person. Not that I'm all that great now, but I was really into myself back then. I'm sure that's why your mother didn't want to tell you anything about me."

Ian could see Jane's face soften. "My mom didn't really say anything bad about you. She just said you had a busy job and couldn't be around."

"It's a sad thing, but I don't even remember your mother. Even if I saw her, I'm not sure I'd recognize her. It was a terrible thing I did. I helped create you and then abandoned my creation. Maybe the worst thing I've ever done in my life." Ian could feel tears beginning to accumulate on his neck.

A nurse walked in, smiled, and said something in Japanese. Her smile grew awkward as she noted both Ian and Jane were crying. It grew even more awkward when they failed to answer. She politely bowed and left the room.

Ian wiped his face with his sleeve. "What does your mother do?"

"She works in a grocery store," Jane replied, matter-of-factly. "She's worked there since I was little. Had a couple boyfriends. One was a pretty good guy. The other was reprobate."

"Do you have any siblings?"

"No, it was just me and Mom. We didn't have much, but we did okay."

"Where did you grow up?"

"Oakland. South side."

Ian sat up, noticing his back seemed to hurt less. "Why did you leave when you saw the letter?"

Jane was quiet for a moment. "I thought you'd be disappointed. I didn't think you'd want me."

Ian held his hands out. "Why would you think that?"

"I don't know. I just figured you wouldn't want me to be your daughter."

Ian slowly twisted himself to the side of the bed. He pulled himself to his feet, wincing. He gingerly stepped across the room. He stood in front of Jane and put his hands on her cheeks. "I am thrilled you are my daughter. And I hope to make up for all the time I've lost not being your father."

Jane jumped to her feet and threw her arms around Ian. Sobbing, she held Ian tightly for several minutes. Ian hugged her back.

When she let go Ian collapsed on the floor.

––––––––––––

When Sy and the two bands arrived at the hospital, they met a flustered pair of nurses, replete in their white uniforms, cornetts, and gloved hands.

"Where are they?" Sy shouted.

One of the nurses bowed and shook her head. The other held up her hands and said something in Japanese that Sy couldn't understand.

"They've got to be here somewhere!" Rod said and started to walk down the Emergency Room hall, peeking into patient rooms.

A large, bald man wearing a short-sleeve shirt and tie appeared. He stood in front of Rod and waved a finger. He said something in Japanese that was very direct. Rod understood from the tone he was being told to stop and return to the entrance.

A doctor appeared a moment later. "What's going on here?" he said in English with a slight Texas drawl.

"We're looking for Jane Miller," Steve replied.

"We don't have a Jane Miller here," the doctor noted.

"Oh God, she couldn't give them her name," Sara said, looking as if she were going to cry.

"She's about five-foot-three, has sandy brown hair" Sy pointed to Indira. "And about her age."

"We don't have a patient like that here, but there is a young woman accompanying another patient. Tall fella with long black hair."

Sy and the bands were silent for a moment. Finally, Sy asked, "The tall fellow is the patient?"

"Yes, ma'am" the doctor replied.

"Oh God, she tried to kill Ian," Kara said, shaking her head.

"Where are they?" Sy asked.

"Well, let me see if they're okay talking to ya'll," The doctor motioned for the group to stay where they were and then disappeared around a corner.

Steve looked at the bald man with the tie. "They really shouldn't be left alone together. If she tried to kill him once, she'll probably try again." The bald man didn't respond.

A few moments later the doctor returned.

"It seems they're okay seeing ya'll."

The band members followed the doctor to the back of the Emergency Department. As they entered the exam room, Ian was seated on a gurney. Jane sat next to him.

Rod cleared his throat. "Well, gosh, I'm glad to see you both."

"Thank you. We're fine," Jane replied.

"You're clearly not fine. You ran away and now we're in a hospital," Sara said, crossing her arms. "What the heck happened?"

Ian smiled. "No worry, mate. I hurt my back, but now I'm fine."

Jane patted his arm. "Ian's had a lot of muscle relaxants."

Ian put his arm around Jane. "Yeah, lots of muscle relaxants. Quite a lot."

"How did you hurt your back?" Indira asked.

"I fell off a large cat."

"He did," Jane added.

The group was silent. Ian cleared his throat. "I was in a rather elevated position on the cat."

"But sunk into the cushioning," Jane added.

"Yes. It was quite difficult once on the cat to move about as I had sunk into the cushions and could barely move."

Rick scratched his head. "You were sitting on a large cat, stuck between the cushions?"

"Well, the cat was shaped like a bus," Jane noted. "With cushions."

Rod crossed his arm. "Sorry. A bus-shaped cat then. Is that right?"

Ian held out his arms. "Exactly. I'm sure it now makes perfect sense."

"And where was Jane during all of this?" Sara asked.

"Oh, I was sitting on the cat, too. The cat that looked like a bus," Jane replied.

"But you weren't stuck in the cushions?" Rod inquired, his arms still crossed.

"No, I was just sitting in the back."

"Of the cat that looked like a bus? The same bus that Ian fell off and hurt his back?"

"Yes."

Sy waved her hands. "Okay, I don't care how you fell, or about whatever it was you fell from or whether you're hallucinating. What I need you to focus on is whether you can sing tonight. Can you get onstage and perform?"

"But of course," Ian said as he started to get up, but his legs began to buckle and Jane grabbed his arm to steady him before he could fall.

"Must be the bloody muscle relaxants. They'll wear off in a few hours," Ian said.

Sy closed her eyes. "I don't think that's going to work."

Rod sighed. "We could cancel."

Sy shook her head. "No. Everything has been ready to go for months. There isn't any contingency for this kind of thing. We'll lose a huge amount of money. The Japanese government won't be nice about it either. There are laws here about remuneration. It isn't clear what we'll be forced to do to make up for the loss."

"And there will be lots of angry fans," Steve added.

The room was silent for a few moments as Sy, Stygian Teal, and Uncle Joe's Band considered what might happen if they weren't able to perform.

Jane broke the silence. "I'll do it."

"Do what?" Sy asked.

"I'll sing. I'll fill in for him," Jane replied.

The room grew silent again. Rod shook his head. "No. It would be too difficult."

Rick grimaced. "Yeah, you'd have to get through all our songs. The lyrics, getting the sound just right, it would be nearly impossible."

"If you'd had time to practice, to learn the lyrics, maybe," Steve added. "But going on cold. That's impossible."

Jane smiled. "How many weeks have I been listening to you guys? How many times have I heard your songs? Give me a prompter of some kind and I'll do it."

"But what about our set?" Sara asked. "You'd have to play our set and then go on again with the guys. That's a lot of vocals."

Ian tried standing again. He began to lean to one side before Rick was able to catch him. As he sat, he ran his hand through his hair. "I know you're all skeptical. But she can do it. She can pull this off." He put his hand on Jane's shoulder. "She's tougher than you think."

Sy stepped in front of Jane and stared directly into her eyes. "If you try this, it can't be halfway. You can't start and then decide not to finish, no matter how bad you sound or if you forget some lyrics or anything else goes wrong. You have to finish. Not finishing isn't an option."

"I understand," Jane replied.

"You don't. Which is why I'm telling you all this. Not finishing isn't an option. Just to be clear."

Sy turned to Ian. "You're okay with this? To an extent your career is on the line here. This doesn't work and it's going to be tough to get you back to a venue like this."

Ian nodded. "I'm good with it."

"Why?" Rod asked. "Why are you so certain this will work? Why are you okay doing this?"

Ian put his hand on Jane's arm. "Because she's my daughter. It's in her blood."

———————————

At the Tokyo Budokan a few hours before the show, the bands felt an intensity that they hadn't in the past. Stygian Teal began to run through their pre-performance practice. After they'd tuned their instruments and played a few riffs from the first few songs, Allison held up her hand.

"You know, one way we could help Jane is if we sang a few of her songs. Would give her voice more time to decompress before she starts into Uncle Joe's Band's lyrics."

Jane shook her head. "No. It's all right. I got this."

"I'm sure you do but let us help you a bit. It isn't going to hurt if we take a bit of the weight of these songs off you," Indira added.

"Yeah. I can sing the main part of 'Twisted Alliance,' Sara can sing 'Revealed,' and Allison can do 'Just Now.'" Kara said as she set her guitar back on the stand.

Jane hesitated for a moment. "Well, okay. I'm not sure how I feel about someone else singing my lyrics, but I guess it makes sense."

Kara cleared her throat. "First, they aren't your lyrics, they're ours. Secondly, it isn't the whole show. It's just a few songs to keep you a bit more rested. Third, it gives us a chance to help, which we would very much like to do."

Jane sighed. "Understood. You guys do those songs. I'll save a bit more for the second show."

Offstage Rick and Steve watched. Rick spoke to Steve in a low voice. "This isn't going to work, is it?"

"Probably not," Steve replied. "I'm not worried about her remembering the lyrics, though. It's Ian's range that's the problem."

Rick nodded. "Yeah. Even if we pare down the song list, she'd still have to hit nearly five octaves."

Steve sighed. "Well, it's been a good run. Figured we'd flame out at some point. Just didn't think it'd be at a show in Tokyo."

"It has been a good run, hasn't it?"

———————

As Jane stood on stage with Uncle Joe's Band, Sy could feel herself breathing faster. She spoke into a mike whose sound reverberated through the speakers on either side of the stage. "Jane. Okay, Jane, listen up. The lyrics are going to be on three different prompters just in front of the stage. I want you to make sure you read the prompters, okay? Whatever you do, just read the prompters."

Jane waved her hand and nodded. She picked up a mike and waited for Uncle Joe's Band to start playing. Rod opened with a riff, which was followed by the addition of Steve's drums and Rick's bass. The song began on a low note and gradually grew, rising from a deep guttural sound to one that shook the rafters. By the time the vocals began the sound was deafening.

As Jane started the first lyric her voice was drowned out but the instrumentalists. After a few moments Rod held up his hand and the band stopped playing. He grimaced and shook his head. "This isn't working," he mouthed to Sy.

Jane stopped singing and turned around, unsure what to do. Allison walked across the stage and stood in front of her.

"This isn't going to work if you hold back," Allison said.

Jane sighed. "I'm not sure I can do this. I don't think my voice is big enough."

"This isn't a punk thing. This is metal. It's all raw emotion. You have to be open enough to be willing to scream as much as sing. When they play, let it rip. Loud. Think *loud*." Allison turned to the band. "Start again. This time let her build her way into the song."

Rod shrugged. He began the guitar riff again, followed by the bass and drums. As Jane started to sing, she dropped her voice an octave and let it rise with the increasing intensity of the music. By the time she reached the chorus she had matched the sound.

CHAPTER 21

Into the Budokan

Famous everyday
A favorite, loud songs loves
After the father

—Jo Ojisan

Fans streamed into the arena an hour before the show began. In the dressing rooms the two bands prepared, putting on stage makeup, tuning their instruments, and warming up their voices. In the Stygian Teal dressing room, Jane sat by herself while the others chatted.

Allison, who had continued to work as a stagehand while playing the guitar with Stygian Teal, burst through the door a half hour before the show was to start. "Are we ready?"

Sara replied, "Yes, we are."

Sara, Kara, and Indira stood and began to move toward the dressing room door. Jane remained seated. Allison held up her hand. "Jane, are you ready?"

Jane took a deep breath. "I don't know if I can do this."

Sara put her hand on Jane's shoulder. "You got us here. You can do this."

"Yeah, we wouldn't even be a band if it weren't for you," Indira added.

Allison smiled. "There isn't anything you can't do. You've done this all before. Just do it again."

Jane closed her eyes. "I never thought I'd be here. I'm going to perform with my sisters and then I'm going to perform with a famous band in place of my father. It's a lot."

Kara smiled. "Don't forget, you're about to have the most fun you've ever had."

Allison put her arm around Jane. "Yeah. In the end this is all about having fun. You sing because you like to sing. So go out there and sing."

Jane stood, hugged each of her bandmates, and led them to the stage.

———————————

The show started with the lights onstage nearly off. Then, in an explosion designed to shock both visual and auditory senses, the stage exploded with bright stage lights and the sounds of Stygian Teal.

Jane sang the first two songs but picked up a guitar for the third and forth as Sara and Allison sang. During the fifth song her voice dropped an octave before she raised it during the last chorus. By the end of the set her voice still seemed in good form and she appeared to have more than ample energy to continue with Uncle Joe's Band.

Stygian Teal stepped off stage to thunderous applause. Jane made her way to Uncle Joe's Band's dressing room where Rod, Steve, and Rick were huddled together. As she walked in, they stopped talking and Rod motioned for her to join the group.

"Okay, here's how we're going to handle this. I'm going to introduce you and let the audience know that Ian's been injured and can't be with us tonight, so you're filling in. I'll just put it out there and hopefully it will go over well with the crowd." He paused. "So don't come on stage until I introduce you."

Jane nodded.

"Then, once we start, you're going to be able to see the lyrics on the monitor. At any point, if you don't think you can sing, if your voice just runs out of gas or anything else happens, I want you to turn to me or Rick and put your hand up by your mike. That'll be the signal for us to jump in and start singing."

Jane put her hand by her nose. "You mean like this?"

Rod shook his head. "No, more like this." He put his hand on the side of his face.

Jane nodded. "Got it. And what if something happens and I don't notice it? Like my pitch falters, or the lyrics are off and I don't notice."

"You'll hear a loud guitar riff," Rod replied. "If there's a riff out of place, or it seems to overwhelm your vocals, stop singing and turn around."

"Yes, if it doesn't make sense, just stop," Rick added.

As the group turned toward the door, Steve took Jane by the arm. "Remember, this is a band. A group. You aren't alone."

When Uncle Joe's Band took the stage Rod played a short guitar riff and then stepped up to the mike. "Good evening, Tokyo!" The crowd responded with applause. "Today our lead singer had a bit of an accident. Ian wanted to sing tonight and I'm sure if he could find a way, he would love to perform for all of you. Since he can't, and because we really wanted to play in Tokyo, we found a backup. You all just heard her sing with Stygian Teal. Here she is, Jane Miller!" Rod stopped and began another slow guitar riff and Jane made her way to the front of the stage. She waved at the crowd. She couldn't tell if there was modest applause or booing while Rod carried on with his solo. As he ended, Rick began a slow rumble on the bass, signaling the beginning of the next song. As it grew in pitch, Jane began to sing.

> *Don't need no prince, no castle too*
> *Don't need no dress, you wasted fool*
> *I'm my own fairy godmother*
> *I'll get my own ride, to the prince's ball*
> *Keep your happy ending, I'll take the fall.*
>
> *Break the glass slipper*
> *Break the glass slipper*
>
> *Don't need no prince, I'm made of stone*
> *Keep your carriage, I walk alone*
> *Go tell stepmother*
> *She's a slave, she's a witch*
> *I'm going to go now, scratch an itch*
>
> *Break the glass slipper*
> *Break the glass slipper*

Much to her own surprise, her voice held during the peak part of the song, able to manage the increased range and sound. She briefly looked across the stage at Rick, who nodded to her approvingly.

After three songs, Rod sang the fourth, after which the band paused. Jane stepped in front of the crowd. "How are y'all doing tonight?" She yelled. The crowd yelled. "We've been in Japan for the last few weeks and we love it here. You are the most bad-assed fans anywhere in the world!" The crowd yelled again.

Jane began to sing the band's ode to commercialism:

> *When nature melds the sun and rain into a giant arch*
> *That stretches from the heavens to the ground, and runs from*
> *light to dark*
> *A man has come from far away to steal the heaven's spark*
> *He takes the colored glory thinking he can find a way.*
> *To build a rainbow out of dirt and sawdust and clay.*
>
> *Chasing gold at the end of the rainbow*
> *Chasing gold at the end of the rainbow*
> *Chasing gold at the end of the rainbow?*
>
> *The man sells rainbow colors to anyone who pays*
> *He makes the factory rainbow, and sells it away*
> *The sky is dark and colorless*
> *There is no beauty left to see*

At the end of the song Jane held up her hand. Rod and Rick put down their guitars and huddled with her.

"What's up?" Rod asked.

"I don't think my voice is going to hold out much longer. It's starting to break in the higher octaves." Jane touched her throat.

Rod turned to Rick. "We can try and buy some time. Maybe you or I will sing the next one?"

Rick nodded. "Yeah, we can, but there's a lot of concert left to go. We can sing the next few songs, but we can't do a whole show."

Rod turned to Jane. "Okay, you sit the next two songs out and then see where we are after that."

Jane looked at Rick. "What do I do?"

"Just hold one of the extra guitars and pretend to play. You can mouth some words as well."

Jane took a deep breath. She walked to the back of the stage and was handed a guitar by one of the stagehands. As Rod began to play the next song she strummed and mouthed a few of the words.

Rod sang "The Bat in the Attic," a lyrically simplistic song, but one that lent itself to a lengthened period of singing and guitar riffs. By the time he was done the song had lasted nearly fifteen minutes.

When Rod finished singing, Rick began a slow grind on his bass. Steve slowly joined on the drums. Rod began a riff on his guitar. The music built over several minutes. Rick started to sing in a low voice. Rod joined in. Jane continued to pretend to sing.

After Rick concluded singing, Rod sang "Under the Gaze," then both turned back toward Jane who handed her guitar back to the stagehand and proceeded toward a mike. She nodded at Rod who looked at Steve and Rick and signaled to start the next song, "Agent Man."

The song began with a drum solo and guitar hook. The first lyrics, "When the time has come for me to sing," began with Jane starting an octave lower than either Rick or Rod expected. They quickly changed their guitars' crescendo to accommodate. After the first lyric the song necessitated a loud scream from the vocalist. Jane opened her mouth to let loose her voice. Instead of a loud roar a tepid growl emerged. Rod looked backstage to see if there was a problem with Jane's mike. One of the stagehands shrugged and pointed at Jane.

As the song continued Jane's mouth opened but nothing that sounded like music, nor like a human voice at any pitch, came out. Quickly, Rod began to increase the intensity of his guitar playing, but he knew he could only last for so long. Jane stopped singing and turned to look backstage. She could see Sy with her arms raised, trying to say something. As Rod's riff came to an end, Jane tried again to open her mouth but nothing came out. Her face grew red with embarrassment. Steve and Rick continue to play, hoping for a miracle.

Jane's head dropped as she imagined her career coming to an end. She could see the Tik-Tok videos, the reports on TMZ and the article on page six. For the briefest of moments, she wondered why she had ever agreed to go on tour.

As Jane's head dropped, Rod shot Rick a look of desperation. Rick glanced backstage. He could see Sy with her hands out. Kara and Sara had a look of horror on their faces.

Then the catcalls began. At first a few sputtered from various corners. Slowly they merged into a loud, sputtering groan.

Amid the boos Jane opened her mouth to sing. Even though no words emerged, a voice blared from the speakers in the great auditorium. Jane looked up. Rod, Rick, and Steve continued to play as the voice continued.

From the darkness backstage a figure shuffled toward the band. Rick was the first to recognize the voice. He smiled as Ian, resplendent in black leather, his signature Lennonesque sunglasses and a new silver and black cane gradually made his way toward the front of the stage. With the mike in his right hand, he held himself up with the cane in his left.

The catcalls rapidly turned to cheers. By the time the song ended most of the crowd was standing.

Rod looked at Ian. "You remember Billy Idol in the '90s, don't you?"

Ian held up his cane. "I got an exact replica, mate."

Jane pointed to her throat. She mouthed, "My voice is gone."

Ian put his arm around her shoulder. "No worries, love. Just grab a guitar. I'm so full of muscle relaxants I can sing all night."

Jane mouthed, "I thought you couldn't be here tonight. Why are you here?"

Ian smiled. "I wasn't going to leave my daughter out here all alone."

CHAPTER 22

Ichi-go, Ichi-e
一期一会

The eternal wind
Blown by the sound of the band
Makes heaven listen

—Jo Ojisan

Like many things in Japan, the most famous saying in Japanese is remarkable for both its simplicity and complexity. The phrase "Ichi-go, Ichi-e" literally means "one time, one meeting." But the simplicity of the phrase should not suggest that the idea it conveys is small.

Every moment and every interaction we have with others is its own unrepeatable event. The time we have with others, the seconds we spend together are sacred and each individual one cannot and will not ever be repeated. "Once in a lifetime" isn't merely those moments we are inclined to celebrate and remember, but literally every minute we are alive.

The phrase is thought to have arisen from a sixteenth-century tea ceremony master who extolled the idea that meeting one's host should be treated as a once-in-a-lifetime event. Even though the host and guest may see each other in other gatherings, each singular event will never be repeated exactly like the others before.

While it may be true that every moment is its own special event and that every meeting is a singular experience never to be exactly repeated, there are those encounters that have a ripple effect, changing the course of time, altering the future in ways those involved cannot imagine, well beyond the purview of their own lives.

It is hard to know when exactly these instances will occur or who will be affected, but they are often a nexus between one epoch and the next, a singular instance with the power to change lives far, far beyond the confines of those immediately involved.

Such a moment occurred on January 24, 1970.

———————

The Grateful Dead seldom played outside the confines of the United States. Of their nearly 2,300 shows, only a few dozen were not within the continental US, and the majority of those that weren't were in Canada and Europe. Some have suggested they were an American phenomenon that simply couldn't be translated elsewhere. Others reckon stringent drug laws compelled the band to avoid overseas exhibition.

Though not quite overseas, in 1970 the Dead played a notable concert at the Civic Center in Honolulu, Hawaii. It was a raucous show, recorded and released in full years later. The impact of Hawaii proved important to Jerry Garcia, who vacationed there often in his later years. It has been noted by some that one of Jerry's favorite pastimes was scuba diving in the pristine waters around Oahu.

Yet the most notable event at the Grateful Dead concert in Hawaii wasn't the concert itself, the release of a recording, or even Jerry donning a wetsuit. Rather it was a meeting that took place somewhere in the dark confines of the Honolulu Civic Auditorium.

———————

Uncle Joe had never traveled on a plane or a boat, save for a ride he took across Lake Tahoe on a small sailboat to the Tahoe Mushroom Company, which, much to his chagrin, proved to be little more than a resource for high-end restaurants. Despite his lack of seaworthy experience, in 1970 he boarded a freighter headed for Hawaii in hopes of seeing the Grateful Dead play a show in Honolulu.

The captain of the ship initially thought Joe would fill the role of a deckhand, until it became clear that Joe's primary interest was standing on the railing near the front of the ship "riding a really big board."

Once in Hawaii, Joe made his way to Waikiki Beach where he

slept beneath a banyan tree for nearly a day before making his way to the auditorium. He woke to the sight of a small crowd of tourists gathered around him, pointing, and taking pictures. It wasn't until he noticed that a seal had come ashore, made its way to the banyan tree, and apparently found Joe a suitable sleeping companion, it's back to Joe and flipper cast over his leg. When Joe awoke it immediately began to scurry back toward the sea, no doubt confused why its soft, smelly pillow had suddenly moved. Joe took it as a sign the concert would be starting soon (why else would the seal leave) and he should find his way to the concert hall.

At most Grateful Dead concerts Joe would lazily make his way to the front of the crowd, talk his way past security (without a ticket), slip forward until he was near the stage, pull out a large joint, light it, and blissfully absorb the music. He knew most of the stagehands and roadies who helped set the stage and would occasionally be let into the inner recesses of wherever the Dead happened to be performing.

Honolulu wasn't, however, like most Dead concerts. The band had hired an outside stage management company to help set up, provide crowd control, and ensure the show went on as planned. Arriving early, Joe managed to skirt the crowd that had lined up to enter the Civic Auditorium.

While he loitered near the entrance waiting for a moment to slip past security, Joe noticed a young man wearing an oversized Hawaiian shirt and neatly pressed shorts. The young man appeared out of place next to the long-haired, scantily dressed crowd.

Joe sidled next to him. "Hey, man. You look familiar. Are you local?"

The young man looked confused for a moment. "No. I am not local."

"Oh. Where are you from?"

The young man paused before answering. "From Sapporo. In Japan."

"Yeah. Cool, man. I kind of thought you might be Japanese. I'm Joe. What's your name?"

"I am Joji. It is a pleasure to meet you."

"That's super cool. I'm Joe. You're Joji. It's like we're the same guy."

Joji nodded in a way that suggested he only partially understood what Joe had said.

As they approached the ticket takers at the entrance, Joji pulled out a ticket. Joe stood behind him. As Joji handed the ticket to a woman tearing stubs off tickets Joe slipped past him and into the arena. The moment the woman looked up, all she saw was Joji holding his hand out waiting for a ticket. She took it and tore off the stub, wondering what she had missed.

When Joji entered the arena, he found Joe waiting for him. "Joji, is this the first Grateful Dead concert you've been to?"

Joji smiled. "Yes. I am very excited. I have heard they are a very good musical band."

Joe put his arm around Joji. "Joji, my new Japanese friend, this is far more than a very good musical band. This is an *experience*."

"Oh, an experience. That sounds very exciting." Joji looked at his ticket. "Where do we sit, Joe-san? I don't see a seat number on the ticket."

"Seats are for people who are tied down. They're for people who have to be in the same place. We don't need a number, man."

"I understand. No numbers. This is a very good way to experience it."

Joe nodded. He pointed to the stage. "Follow me, Joji. It's time to find a new reality."

"Time to be tall."

Joe looked at Joji, who was at least six inches shorter. "Not sure we're going to grow."

"Yes, time to see from a tall place."

"Ohhh.... Time to get high. Joji, you are my man."

Joji followed Joe as he slipped through the crowd and made his way to the stage. Joji thought for a moment that Joe must be some sort of celebrity, as the other fans reached out to shake Joe's hand, pat him on the back or ask what Joe had done with their stash.

When they reached the stage, Joe looked for someone who might direct him backstage. The usual cacophony of security guards and roadies weren't familiar so Joe had to barter with a rather large fellow wearing sandals and a green security shirt to get backstage. As he made his way past a barrier at the edge of the stage, Joe pulled Joji behind him.

While Joe and Joji snuck backstage, the Grateful Dead stepped onstage to loud applause and began to tune their instruments. The band began a short rendition of "Franklin's Tower" as Joe found a crate for him and Joji to sit on. Joji's eyes widened as he heard the first song. Joe pulled a joint out of his pocket along with a lighter. He lit it, took a puff, and handed it to Joji.

Joji, without thinking, took a puff from the joint and coughed. "This is the worst cigarette I've ever had."

"A couple more puffs and it'll be the best," Joe replied. He handed it back to Joji. "Trust me."

Joji took another puff. After a few minutes he started to laugh. "Yes, Joe-san, this is a very good cigarette."

For the next hour Joe and Joji watched the Dead from their backstage seats. At one point Jerry looked at the pair, nodded, and smiled.

The Grateful Dead played a long version of Ripple. Joji sat transfixed, humming the words. He looked at Joe. "These words are like a poem."

"Yes, they are very poetic. That's the great thing about the Dead. It's poetry. Like hearing a powerful poem read out loud. Only in a song. Being sung." Joe laughed, not sure what he had just said.

"Joe-san, I mean the words to this song, the part in the middle, the part they sing over and over again, it's like a poem."

"You mean the chorus. That part."

"Yes, it is a poem."

Joji hummed,

> *Ripple in still water*
> *When there is no pebble tossed*
> *Nor wind to blow*

"You see, Joe-san. It is a poem. A *haiku* poem."

Joe thought for a moment, remembering the five-seven-five syllable makeup of haiku poems. He counted. "Whoa, man, you're right. It *is* a haiku."

They both sat silently for a few minutes.

Joe tapped Joji on the arm. "Dude, you should be a poet. Just like the Dead. A *haiku* poet."

When Uncle Joe's Band left Japan, they had found a new well of

171

creative energy. Songs that once felt tired, suddenly became alive. Lyrics that had felt clunky were reimagined in ways that made them poignant and clever. Guitar and drum riffs were woven together into an ethereal carpet of sound. Every day was the start of a newly creative endeavor.

As the band's skills and sound grew, so did their audience. Sy found herself doing less to sell the band's music to recording companies than fielding their inquiries about future contracts. As sales increased, the band members found themselves performing in ever larger venues on a less frequent basis. As they became less accessible their popularity grew even more. Instead of hocking household consumer products they were asked to write scores for movies and make music videos.

Several times on subsequent tours they made their way back to Japan, where they reminisced about game shows, vending machines, and Godzilla. On nearly every visit Sy would ensure that they played at least one show at the Tokyo Budokan, where Ian would perform either a capella or with Rod playing an acoustic guitar. Longtime band watchers invariably found these to be Uncle Joe's Band's best performances.

How and when Joji Kinosara died is unknown. By the time he had entered the throes of late middle age he had lost touch with family, friends, and anyone else who had ever known him. How long he continued to drive his Subaru van throughout Japan is a matter of complete speculation. Whether he met his demise in the farthest reaches of the islands or in a hospital bed unknown to those caring for him remains a mystery.

Less uncertain was the final whereabouts of his van, seen and collected by the national vehicle registry on a lone stretch of road north of Sapporo. The van was unoccupied, appeared to have been lived in for many years, and contained little to suggest where its owner might have gone. A thorough search revealed only a registration card signed by Joji's father, long since deceased, a hat with "United States Marine Corp" emblazoned on it, and a notebook filled with poetry.

The public never discovered the identity of Jo Ojisan, though scholars were able to pinpoint the last time he had scribbled a haiku on a landmark. Unsure what had become of him, they speculated he had simply grown too old, or too tired to continue writing poetry. His life was never celebrated, his disappearance never mourned, but books of his haikus line the shelves of bookstores to this day. A few of the objects on which he wrote made their way into the National Museum of Contemporary Art, where they have been carefully preserved.

Popular myth has it that the character who wrote beautiful haiku in the most public of places may still be making his way among the populace, stopping occasionally to marvel at a flower or have dinner with an unsuspecting host. "Welcome the uncle's words" became a famous phrase, meaning that one should be hospitable to strangers, lest they be the infamous wandering poet.

In the end it may be most appropriate to imagine Joji Kinosara and the poet Basho searching throughout Japan for the best view of the mid-summer's moon, never quite satisfied, but never deterred.

Uncle Joe's Band was famous and well regarded by both critics and record labels. They played in venues large and small, to crowds of all ages, across the globe.

The members of Uncle Joe's Band were contemplative and insightful. They would speak to reporters humbly of their roots, the sources of their musical inspiration, and the positive messages they hoped their fans would take away from their songs and lyrics. Often, when asked what role in life they found most meaningful, they would mumble something about their role as fathers and mentors, careful to acknowledge that they hadn't always appreciated the fulfillment that came from helping others.

At many of their shows, Uncle Joe's Band was preceded by the female punk band Stygian Teal, whose musical abilities and lyrical work grew with the passage of time. The five young women who made up the band were at once precocious and wise, poignant and frivolous, exuberant and staid. Their songs were said to be eclectic, though that may have reflected the uninteresting and plagiaristic nature of popular music more than anything particularly unusual about Stygian Teal.

On occasion, hints of Uncle Joe's Band's unique sound could be detected in Stygian Teal's music, as though some echo of words or melody or feeling had been passed from one band to the other. Critics never remarked about the connection, nor entertained the idea that the older, all-male metal band might somehow have influenced the musical aspirations of the younger female punk rockers. Regardless of the oversight, they would often find themselves using the same adjectives when describing the two groups.

To anyone who saw the bands together, the affection between them was apparent. The men in Uncle Joe's Band coached, cheered, consoled, and challenged, always seeming to revel in the successes of their younger colleagues and mourn their failures. In turn, the women of Stygian Teal listened and learned, sought counsel and approval, ever genuinely interested in the guidance of the older group.

It is said that true families are not born of blood, but of respect and joy for one another's lives. By that measure Stygian Teal and Uncle Joe's Band were as much a family as any other. To be sure, there were at times rifts between the bands and their members. Such is the nature of all families. But in the end the ties that bound them were stronger than the fractious forces pulling them apart, and the discord that had so punctuated their unfortunate lives alone had been made harmonious together.

Real poetry is to lead a beautiful life.
To live poetry is better than to write it.
— Matsuo Basho

Thank you to my friends and fellow writers in Novelitics and PDX Writers. It's wonderful to have a community with whom to commiserate, console, celebrate, and consider.

Additionally, thank you to the Oya No Kai community at Portland Public Schools. More than a few incidents in *Uncle Joe's Senpai* were based on occurrences during visits to Japan. And thanks to Robert and Bettina Ishimaru in whose classes I have the honor of playing the role of a senpai.

A few words about haiku…

Poetry has been described as the condensation of novel length material into a few short lines. No better an example can be found than that of the great haiku masters of Japan. For all the beauty of sonnets and elegies, it is the simple haiku that is often most apt at saying so much by saying so little.

The haiku in *Uncle Joe's Senpai* does not (with a couple exceptions) follow the most traditional haiku form. The most structured haiku follows the 5-7-5 syllable format, and includes a *kereji* (a word that underlies the structure and closes the poem) and *kigo* (reference to a season). As with any translation from one language to another the depth of meaning can be lost simply due to the underlying structure of the language itself. The concept of *kereji*, for example, doesn't have an exact equivalent in English, nor does the syllabic meter with which words in English are measured translate perfectly into Japanese. Further complicating (or confusing) a traditionalist's approach to translating haiku are the differences between a phonetic alphabet and one that includes logographic characters.

For the purposes of a novel written in English, the haikus have followed a 5-7-5 syllabic pattern and often there is a reference to a season, but little else consistent with the traditional structure. Hopefully, dear reader, you will still find them humorous and interesting.

Made in the USA
Las Vegas, NV
26 July 2023

75246384R00105